# SCHELDESTROOM

## A Century of Sailing Adventure in Resilience, Courage Fun and Determination.

*Een eeuw zeilavontuur in veerkracht, moed, plezier en vastberadenheid.*

### KEITH PAULUSSE

# SCHELDESTROOM

# SCHELDESTROOM

A Century of Sailing Adventure in Resilience, Courage, Fun and Determination

*Een eeuw zeilavontuur in veerkracht, moed, plezier en vastberadenheid*

## KEITH PAULUSSE

**ARPress**
45 Dan Road Suite 5
Canton MA 02021

Hotline: 1(800) 220-7660
Fax:      1(855) 752-6001


Ordering Information:
Quantity sales. Special discounts are available on quantity purchases by corporations, associations, and others. For details, contact the publisher at the address above.

Printed in the United States of America.

ISBN-13:    Paperback      979-8-89389-263-5
                  eBook          979-8-89389-264-2

Library of Congress Control Number:    2024907677

# Scheldestroom Chapter Summaries

INTRODUCTION

- Historical resources and records
- Scheldestroom Research Team members

CHAPTER 1

- The van Aalst sisters working in London
- Dutch directness in communication with the English
- Meeting *Emmeline Pankhurst*, a leader of the British Suffragette and writer *Virginia Woolf.*
- Attending shows at the west end she talked about Oscar Wilde's *The Importance of Being Ernest.*
- London Department stores were a "Paradise for ladies".
- Meeting Mr. Boot a shipsbuilder of fast graceful Klippers.

CHAPTER 2

- The three Paulusse bros visited the 1900 World Fair/ 'Paris Exposition Universelle',
- The bros returned from Paris excited and repurposed,
- Experience made them visionaries, innovators, entrepreneurs and critical thinkers
- The journey from Terneuzen to Delft took almost four hours, with them they carried a cash deposit of 1500 guilders.
- From February to November 1911 the *Scheldestroom* plied the tidal rivers of the transporting bricks.
- Kees and Francine visited the nearby hennep growing fields cultivated by the manufactures of hemp products
- Children born on The Scheldestroom.

# CHAPTER 3

- The Great War begins. The Netherlands remains neutral.
- Scheldestroom rescuing Belgian Refugees.
- The van Aalst sisters volunteer at the Hontenisse Refugee camp.
- British Brigade carried by Scheldestroom to internment camps.
- Francine took the steering wheel, and Kees set full sails catching the maximum winds, outracing the minesweeper,
- Allied planes landing at Cadzand.
- No Paulusse children born during that war, birth control practiced.

# CHAPTER 4

- The roaring twenties when Scheldestroom roared
- Prosperity and new technology
- The births of three sons
- Bricks for the IX Olympics in Amsterdam
- Klippers; *Scheldestroom* and the *Elizabeth* sailing in tandem
- Paulusse bros caring for disabled family and friends
- Creativity, tenacity Recondition car engine placed in sloops

# CHAPTER 5

- The 1930 Depression. Scheldestroom laid up.
- Smugling potatoes to designated secret warehouses.
- Destruction by Netherlands Goverment of mountains of fresh produce.
- Scheldestroom becomes boat building yard
- Alternative business founded
- Prosperity continues.

# CHAPTER 6

- Almost bombed out of existence at Hansweert.
- Jan-Pieter Paulusse hit by shrapnel.

# INTRODUCTION

## The Scheldestroom historical re sources

When my parents Piet and Bets reached their 60th wedding anniversary, I decided to spend every weekend with them in their house on top of Leopold Hill in Victoria.

Frequently when the weather was nice, we'd go for short road trips, picnics or visiting some of their elderly friends. We'd chat about everything past present and their future destiny. They were always interested in living; they did not fear the future because they had learnt from the past that fear of the imaginary unknown is a heavy psychological burden.

Mum Bets was diagnosed with Alzheimer's five years earlier. She had little or none short-term memory nodules left; her long term memory was intact. Piet had mild Parkinson's, but with medication, the debilitating effects were subdued.

Soon it was necessary that I resign from my job and move in with them as slow deterioration of their condition was evident. For almost three years, I was with them until they passed away. Piet and I talked a lot about his formative years on the ship of his birth de *Scheldestroom,/ Scheldtstream* the depression of the 1930s, the invasion and enemy occupation of the Netherlands, his military service in the Zeeland Battalion 2/14 RI, the Police action in the Indonesia intervention, his love for Bets, the births of his children and of course migrating to Australia.

Bets followed our conversations via the many photo albums of the different periods of the Paulusse detailing our collective family lives. Her long term memory was sharp, so she recalled events quickly once she saw a picture in the photo albums and eagerly partook in the conversations and recalled events.

Besides the photo albums, there were a thousand or so postcards and letters all stacked in several shoeboxes, going back over a hundred years. We'd ploughed through them reread and more than often reliving the good and less beautiful moments. Postcards are like a time capsule of time and space detailing events about the *Scheldestroom* and people that lived on her.

We have a thousand or so books in our library carried from generation to generation. Recently I unearthed even more material that shed light on the *Scheldestroom*. My grandparents and my dad, *I delightfully discovered*, had the habit of putting surprising things in between the book pages. Items such as personal letters, newspaper cuttings and hand-drawn design sketches of the *Scheldestroom* added to my intrigue and motivation. These finds all related to the various periods of the life of the Scheldestroom. I realised then that the *story of the Scheldestroom is a historical thriller* encapsulating the whole of the twentieth century.

A further impetus for writing the Scheldestroom story began when my cousin drew my attention to a ship for sale site in The Netherlands. Lo and behold, there was the 110-year-old Scheldestroom detailed with many pictures. Albeit modernised lengthened and motorised yet still recognisable by her handsome bow and stern. She was sold, and the plan by the new owners is to restore the ship to its former sailing glory.

Every commercial ship in the Netherlands is required to have a cargo manifest Opa/*grandfather* Kees being Dutch kept meticulous records of these and profit loss and expenditure records, I have all of these originals in my possession. When discussing the contents of all these documents with my dad, he had a story for each entry. I jotted down all his recall of memory, not in a dry, dull fashion but with words that expressed the emotion of the times.

In writing Scheldestroom, I used modern sociological, psychological and medical terms that did not exist in 1910. For example; "The van Aalst sisters had a high degree of *emotional intelligence*. And for my grandparent possessed valuable *social capital*, that is, networks of relationships between people with whom they lived in their society, enabling that society to function effectively. Several of my relations in the Scheldestroom story suffered from mental health problems, which I interpreted based on my psychological studies as *bipolar or Aspergers* on the autism spectrum.

The story of the Scheldestroom is adventurous and motivating. It reads like a novel that is told through a *stream of consciousness*, that's my way of telling stories. But it's not a version of a *referential academic book* that forever refers to other literary sources and more sources and the other. No! My story is real and original even ideal because there is nothing terrible or artificially generated sensational drama. But there is excitement and many intrigues such as Kees falling in love with Francine, without this love the Scheldestroom would not have existed. I indeed wouldn't have lived. This story recounts the British navy chasing the Scheldestroom on the river Scheldt during the First World War. The carrying of a thousand Belgian refugees or the transportation of a British naval brigade to Dutch internment camps. The unsuccessful Gestapo seizure of the Scheldestroom. Or the secret construction of a hiding place for Jewish friends. The deconstruction of the Scheldestroom during the Great Depression. An even better question is how a family of ten, eight children and two parents flourished in De Roef/*Ships Cabin*. How did they survive from typhoid and the Spanish flu? How did they get through the difficult times without child support or government social welfare? How did they transport hundreds of tons of cargo across

Western Europe without an engine, only sails and wind power? It all sounds unreal. That's why the story of the Scheldestroom had to be told, it has now been revealed.

Easter time 1968 was the last time I saw my 84 years Opa Cornelis Paulusse. Everybody called him Kees I was named after him as did other grandsons. Before returning to Australia, I spend several days with him cycling through the Zealandic Flanders ancient polders upon their dykes growing giant willows and poplar trees. He took me to historical villages with their aged sanded up harbours. Cycling together to places that were significant in nation-building not only to the Netherland but the world to which the Paulusse family like others had contributed. I say others, but many others did not leave any historical footsteps behind leaving little connection for future generations..

### *Scheldestroom in the Dutch Language - A bilingual book.*

I came to Australia as an eleven-year young boy; my family's spoken language was Zealandic Flemish. Consequent to arriving in Australia in November 1961 my formal Dutch language education came to an abrupt end. However, my book and newspaper reading continued in the Dutch language. At home, we always spoke the Zealand Flanders language changing only when other Dutch people visited then we said the official Dutch language.

I make absolutely no apologies for my 1950's 1960's post-war Dutch immigrant language. With its accompanying Proverbs — Idioms — Sayings — Puns — Aphorisms nor for the vernacular expression for the Zealandic Flemish phrase and prose and presentation as well as syntax which may not conform to accepted Dutch language standards. I find comfort in the assurance to know that I'm m in the good company of fellow Zealandic Flanders writers such as Johan Hendrik van Dale Primary School headmaster at the medieval town of Sluis, whose Lexicography is still the - now three-part - Large Dictionary of the Dutch Language, which is not called that by anyone, but is generally known as the 'Dikke van Dale', and Zealandic Flemish writer and speaker. Then there is Marnix van St Aldegonde who like me spoke Zealandic Flemish and wrote the oldest and continuous National Anthem in the world "Het Wilhelmus" There is something about Zealanders, and their writing consider Jacob Cats a most famous Dutch poet, humorist, jurist and politician. Jacob is known throughout the Netherlands as Father Cats, Poet of the nation. Then there is the more contemporary Annie GM Schmidt, a Zealandic children's writer, playwright of countless musicals. Annie is now included in the "Cannon of Dutch and included Schmidt, alongside national icons such as Vincent Van Gogh and Anne Frank.

## *Scheldestroom research Team*

Louis van der Hooft, Visual storyteller and Oral Historian.

I would not have started writing Scheldestroom without Loius's historical archive containing thousands of historical photographs, postcards, letters, artifacts, film clips of the Zealandic Harbour city of Terneuzen. His collection of significant events about everyday life using audiotapes, video clips, and transcriptions of interviews assisted me enormously. Many times I noticed the Scheldestroom or seen some distant relative participating in an actual historical event involving my ancestors. Viewing Louis exciting archive made me feel connected with the past and gave me the keys to the future.

Andre de Groot

Andre is my second cousin and skipper of a 450-tonne ship the "Unicum" He has chased up historical documents photographs and newspaper articles about Scheldestroom. He also visited and photographed the Scheldestroom at Harlingen shipyard bringing back its original sailing capability.

Patricia Paulusse

My cousin, a fine art artist, and my go-to adviser of all things Dutch. Assisted in reading the Scheldestroom manuscripts made recommendations for improvement


Walter and Elly Hes

This Australian post-war Dutch migrant husband and wife are both writers and authors. They acted as my cheer and encouragement team. They liked the kind of Dutch I spoke and stimulation giving the confidence in writing a dual language book.


Kai Jiang

Portrait Artist; for drawing Francine, and other Scheldestroom moments.

Thanks to *Poolster Charters* at Harlingen The Netherlands for the use of the Poolster River klipper image. www.klipperpoolster.com

# CHAPTER 1



*The van Aalst Sisters.*

*These urbane young van Aalst women from Zealandic Flanders
drew the attention of Sea Captains and Diplomats*

They were sent off to England by their father Jan van Aalst and their friend Cornelis Paulusse, usually called Kees, who sailed them on his 140 tonne wooden cargo *Tjalk* named *De Vertrouwen*, diagonally crossing the choppy and windy waters of the famed Western Scheldt from Terneuzen to Vlissingen/ *Flushing*, a sail journey of 90 minutes against the wind. At Vlissingen they would board a ship to London.

Wednesday, 11th April 1906, was a freezing cold morning when pretty 17 year old Francine together with her attractive older sister Leine boarded the *Prins Hendrik*, a luxurious Paddle Steamer that would sail them to London, taking less than six hours to cross the North Sea. Many of the Zealandic Flanders young women went to work outside their home, even going overseas for adventure as modern 21st century women also do, finding jobs such as process workers, maidservants, and hostesses, bar maids or even brothel madams. They received equal income of their own and they were not dependent so much on the income of their families or husbands; this was the rule in Zealandic Flanders, though not so much elsewhere in The Netherlands where the religious cohorts firmly placed men above women, but usually not in enlightened secular circles.

Francine and Leine had been offered a job on account of their being multilingual and possessing a high degree of *emotional intelligence*, not to mention good looks. Both had a good sense of humour and made everybody feel at ease and included. Their formal education finished at 14 years old and they started work at that young age, beginning as maids. There were six girls in the van Aalst family: Francine, Sophie, Leine, Marie, Lena and Jane, and two brothers, Piet, and handsome Hendrik, the youngest, altogether seven siblings, 11 if counting the three stillborn siblings. They all had descriptive nicknames of endearment. Dad, Jan van Aalst was a low-paid labourer and sometime deckhand, working in a Timber Mill. He married Jana Harte, a milliner. They lived in the neat and tidy neighbourhood called "Java", at Java Straat 32/ *32 Java Street* situated in the Harbour city of Terneuzen, where many of the houses were built by housing collectives of the 19th century.

It didn't matter that the van Aalst family were economically poor; much more importantly they were physically and mentally healthy, evidenced by the fact that most of the siblings lived to an old age. Jan and Janna celebrated their fiftieth wedding anniversary in 1936 at their Java family home amongst their many grandchildren, most of whom feature in the story of the Scheldestroom. I have placed a *foto here* celebrating their anniversary amongst family.

I remember as a child listening to Grandma Francine discussing books with her sibling sisters, all of whom had, throughout their lives, been members of musical theatre performance groups, fine arts societies; consequently they did not suffer from ignorance or prejudice, dullness or lack of creativity or get up and go.

Many of the Zealandic Flanders families were quite sophisticated and possessed much social capital, acquired in the pluralistic, multicultural Harbour community such as Terneuzen being the pivotal point of international activity linking Antwerp, Gent and Bruges, all in a radius of about 35 Kilometre, each of them not only being world renowned harbour cities, but also the spiritual and cultural hubs of Europe for centuries, even at the turn of the 19ᵗʰ century. It was very different in the rest of The Netherlands where people mostly lived in their sectarian bubbles, rarely venturing out of their villages or cities. Antwerp and Ghent are large artistic and literary cultural centres - made famous by the lives such as *Peter Paul Rubens* and *Jan Van Eyck in* Bruges, and *Hugo van der Goes*.

Living in such a multicultural and pluralistic society gave many Zealandic Flanders women a healthy self-confidence and self-worth, developing their intra-personal understanding, unlike the supposed suppression of women elsewhere in Europe and or in the Netherlands.

These urbane young van Aalst women and other women from Zealandic Flanders drew the attention of Sea Captains and Diplomats stationed at these harbour cities including a Charles Van Gyzelen who was Head chef for a while at Hotel Rotterdam in Terneuzen. It was he who recommended Francine and Leine for the domestic supervisor positions and as hostesses for international guests at the soon to be opened Luxurious Ritz Hotel in June 1906. The girls spoke perfect French, English, and German as well as Nederlands. Initially they had already been accepted to start work as domestics for very wealthy English people including the family of the esteemed Lord Kitchener. The rumour had it that Kitchener was not keen on Dutch women or any women for that matter, and preferred the company of young men as servants, besides, the Boer War had just finished five years earlier and the English were still smarting over their recent 65 thousand casualties and 55.000 British soldiers killed, walloped by a rag tag Boer army calling themselves "guerillastrijders". *"Don't forget these Boers are our wayward cousins",* Francine used to tell me with a wink; she got wind of Kitchener's dislike of the Boers and therefore the Dutch so they declined the Kitchener jobs and accepted the positions at the Ritz Hotel. There are many stories about the Ritz in those days but that is not the purpose of this book.

Money a key aspect of going to work besides gaining valuable life experience in London was a significant motivator. Life is mostly is about the importance of the getting of money. They would earn good money; both Kees Paulusse and Francine van Aalst had already secretly discussed marriage without anyone knowing about their intent. Before they'd get married, they decided to save for a decent deposit to have their own ship built, a ship with living quarters with enough comfort and space to start a family. Francine would help by saving her wages.

Francine and Leine were in for a culture shock when they arrived in London. It was so very big and brash. Francine told me that the brashness of city life was softened by the politeness and manners of the English people, very polite, so polite that one never knew where one stood with the English, how they used their language like smoke and mirrors, full of subtleties, euphemisms and idioms; rarely was the spoken word clear or direct. Dutch directness in communication with foreigners regularly caused misunderstandings between the girls from Zeeland and the English. In the first phase of their relationship, she distrusted that very polite speech, afraid that an unpleasant message could be hidden so that they could not discern the intent of the message. Being very nice can raise the suspicion in the minds of the Dutch that someone needs a special favour. Politeness can also cause irritation as it is considered a waste of time. The English liked the Zealand girls but found them awfully direct, calling a spade a spade, using the correct nouns to name things, not a euphemism to hide an unpleasant truth or expression.

Here they were in the English capital, the hub of the strongest power in the world, both economically and militarily. Everything was big in comparison with Terneuzen or Amsterdam, though what it did have in common with Terneuzen was its International shipping from all over the world. That was not so much intimidation or a cultural shock; after all in Terneuzen they had seen and been on board the exciting yachts of King Leopold's *Alberta* or Kaiser Wilhelm's *SMY Hohenzollern II* or even Russia's Tsar Nicholas II's Imperial Yacht, *Standart* when they passed through the Terneuzen to *Gent Chanel* also known as The Sea Channel, matching London in the 1906 roll call of famous ships.

Whilst they were working at the Ritz they met *Emmeline Pankhurst*, a leader of the British Suffragette movement, who talked about social injustices. Emmeline introduced the Dutch girls to a Virginia Stephen who later became the novelist *Virginia Wolf.* Francine said they had so much in common with the English women; the only thing that bothered her was the English class system. Everything was categorised by it in a sort of snobbish, dehumanising way. The van Aalst girls were working class they were told by the English, in a tone and manner sounding like as though that was a disease or affliction, but Francine looked past that and viewed the bigger picture, of what might be the future for women. In the end she said that women were responsible for their own lives and should not be a victim or believe that they should submit themselves totally to man's authority as demanded by conservative religionists. But Francine, like Emily, strongly believed in women getting the vote, but she already felt equal with men in every aspect of life.

They liked going to shows at the west end she talked about Oscar Wilde's *The Importance of Being Ernest.* That was the first time I heard the name *Oscar Wilde,* from Leine. They loved that play as all the pieties of the previous age were turned around and Victorian history and double standards exposed in a funny way. Victorian society was not unlike the *"up-themselves Hollanders"*, but not like Terneuzen. There were no cultural class barriers existing that she was aware of. As she said, *"We're much more exposed to the world of ideas being near the cultural and scientific and industry manufacturing centres of Antwerp, Ghent and Bruges."*

Zealandic Flanders women were not so much subservient to their male counterparts, whether picking potatoes or digging sugar beets or spinning flax in the Zealand Flanders Flax Mills. Women were already equal with men in terms of wages and status, neither were there too many gender specific jobs. A woman could do as good as a man.

The proof of this was that after all they had been ruled by two Dutch Queens, Emma and Wilhelmina, the latter Queen, would rule for most of Francine's life. Wilhelmina was not much older than Francine. They were contemporaries.

As a child in the 1950's Leine told me how they went in the Gigantic Ferris Wheel built in 1894 for the India Exhibition held in London. It was the biggest in the world and the Ferris wheel car in which they were sitting got stuck for two hours. She giggled and said the views were fabulous. One of the other twenty-five passengers they got stuck with in the Ferris wheel car was a Dutch man called Meneer/*Mr* Booth, a steel ship builder from Delft in Nederland.

Even after 50 years Leine showed me Boot's visitor's card, albeit yellowed with age. A few weeks after they were rescued from the Ferris Wheel Saga Mr Booth was invited by the women to come for tea or a Jonge Jenever/ *Dutch Bols Gin* at the Ritz during their day off, primarily because they could speak Dutch with him and Francine could hear him out about his ship building business. Menheer Boot told them that he was looking at shipbuilding techniques in England and Scotland especially the fast Klipper /*Clipper* sailing ships like the *Cutty Sark* - how fast and elegant it was, sailing in a record time of 72 days from Melbourne, Australia, to London. He had in mind a flat steel clipper design built for the inland waterways of Europe. They had to be small enough to zig-zag the narrow channels and river against the wind and also to have enough tonnage to make it viable for the shippers. Menheer Boot wanted to break ground with his new designs. The women would not soon forget this intriguing handsome slightly arrogant and over confident Mr Boot, nevertheless they liked him.

Leine thought the London Department stores were a *"Paradise for ladies"*. A visit was more of a destination, like visiting art galleries or museums or the beach. They were much more than just a big and comprehensively stocked city shop like they had in Terneuzen. For them, these stunning new department stores became places to meet and occasionally have lunch with their English girlfriends. There was so much wonderful panache and drama about these stores, even if they were only window shopping, realising they could not afford to save money and spend money at the same time. Francine, in one of her letters home, wrote how bedazzling department shops like *Selfridges* and *Harrods* were with a hundred departments along with restaurants, a roof garden, reading and writing rooms, reception areas for foreign visitors, a first aid room and, most importantly, a small army of knowledgeable floor-walking assistants who not only served as guides to this retail treasure trove but also thoroughly mingled and were charming in the art of making a sale.

They visited Selfridges Department store one week before they were to travel back to Nederland to purchase small, inexpensive gifts for their siblings and close friends. Much, though, went into gifts such as hand-made crochet handkerchiefs and petite decorative bottles of perfume. Francine purchased an English skipper's sweater, as well as a wool sweater with a turtleneck with buttons for Kees. It was the most expensive of all the gifts. Little did she realise that this gift would be worn nearly every day for twenty years.

After three years their time in England was up, they packed their bags, stored their memories, and practiced their new life skills and sailed back to Terneuzen all excited to tell their stories.

# CHAPTER 2

*The building and birth of the Klipper Scheldestroom.*
*The creation of the Paulusse van Aalst family.*

The North Sea was choppy, caused by a freezing, stiff November breeze, when the van Aalst sisters, Francine and Leine, sailed overnight from London to Vlissingen on the same Paddle Steamer they had sailed on 3 years before. They were sitting in the heated and cosy comfortable deck saloon clutching their hot mugs filled with hot Dutch 'Snert'/ *pea soup* followed later by hot chocolate drinks with almond 'gevulde koeken'/*filled almond cakes* - popular Dutch pastry. It wasn't any secret the van Aalst girls loved their food. They wondered who might meet them on their arrival back at Vlissingen. They had only sent one postcard several weeks ago to their parents, and Francine had written a long letter to Kees, not only advising him about meeting Mr Boot, the ship builder, but also that she had saved 300 guilders, challenging Kees to match her savings, and made a subtle hint about their forthcoming marriage.

The return welcome at Vlissingen was sensational - all 6 sisters and their mother exuding a high-spirited party mood, eagerly waiting for their arrival at the Zeeland Steamboat Terminal, each holding small gifts and bunches of flowers loaded with fragrance. One could be excused for thinking that Royalty was expected to arrive. Kees and his brother, Bram, also waited modestly in the background holding one single red rose. I have to mention here that it is a Dutch cultural phenomenon to give flowers on almost every occasion; it expresses an emotion of empathy without using words. On this occasion they were expressions of a joyous reunion. To everyone's surprise Francine gave Kees big reassuring hugs, and more hugs, tight, tight hugs. She couldn't care less what people would think of her.

Several days after Francine and Leine returned from London they both started work as receptionists again in Hotel Rotterdam in Terneuzen. Kees and his older brother, Bram, began researching what kind of ship he would need to build to ensure that it would support his own future family. This required some critical thinking, not only about efficient designs, but also about economics and competition. It had to be a ship that could carry almost any kind of cargo as well as providing a comfortable home for 40 years.

Their research had begun seven years earlier when Kees and Bram, together with their eldest brother Jacobus, known as Ko, visited the *Paris Exposition Universelle*, commonly known as the World Fair of 1900. This exhibition ushered in and set the tone for new technologies and ideas for the Twentieth Century. Taking the fast steam train at Terneuzen, leaving for Paris at 7 am and arriving there at 4pm, they immediately headed to the famous Paris Eiffel tower, arriving there at 4.30 pm, to try out the newly installed Otis hydraulic lifts before the tower closed at 5 pm. I must note that for most Dutchmen their lives are run by the clock, nearly every minute is accounted for. Ten years later they were still talking about the entry exhibition gate that allowed 60,000 paying visitors entry every hour. Awed with all the new inventions such as talking pictures, electric trams and cars, including the new Diesel engines, electronic escalators, the Telegraphone (a magnetic audio recorder), and X-ray machines. In the Optics Palace they looked at the moon through a very large refracting telescope, enabling them to see the surface of the moon very clearly, then there were the moving sidewalks carrying 1600 people at a time around the pavilions. A new awareness had dawned upon them about rapid changes in technology, globalisation and electronic communications. Production and mass consumption had begun including changes in the social fabric of society. The status of men and women was rapidly equalising, and women received formal education, earning their own money. Madame Marie Curie, together with her husband, were each awarded half of the Nobel Prize for Physics in 1903, for their study into spontaneous radiation. So many inventions had happened in their lifetime, causing them to think seriously about sustainability projected into the future. A new world was taking shape, one filled with experts of all sorts, scientists, statisticians and engineers. The Paulusse brothers returned from Paris excited and repurposed, the residues of their experience having made them visionaries, innovators, entrepreneurs and critical thinkers for years to come.

Tuesday 7 June 1910 at the Terneuzen Town Hall, Kees and Francine were married; theirs was a Civil Marriage. It might be good to mention here that Kees and Francine's future children were not baptized into any religion. They considered church important for people who had no philosophical scope by which to find direction across the hidden paths of life. The Paulusses and the van Aalst were Dutch liberals from the eighteenth century as influenced by the enlightenment of the seventeenth century. Their ideas were to respect people's differences. They were commendable citizens, and emphasized respect for all cultures, religions, and ideologies and the great dictum that we should inclusively love one another unconditionally. Leine would get married in 1915 with 27-year-old Skipper Abraham, known as Bram van Hanegem.

In 1959 Francine and Kees were celebrating their fiftieth wedding anniversary. She gave some advice saying that the secret to love is laughter and not intellectualising emotions too much. Both partners need acceptance, and a big part of this acceptance comes from laughter. Lovers who cannot laugh together about themselves probably aren't very accepting of their relationships. They may not be able to tolerate its unique flaws and inevitable stumbles, any more than they can put up with their own. They say absence makes the heart grow fonder, but they also say, "out of mind, out of heart". Thank goodness that was not the case between Francine and Kees!

For their honeymoon, Kees and Francine travelled to Delft, the city of *Johannes Vermeer*, where they stayed with one of the Francine sisters who was a single mother but had the total love and support of the van Aalst family, although they could not understand why she would live in "Olland" amongst all these self-opinionated, self-righteous Hollanders, but Francine knew why. She told me that the father of her child was a wealthy art dealer in Delft who was married to a Française but said he was an honourable, decent man and kept her sister in a two-storey house, ironically situated only a few kilometres from the ship building company, Boot and Zoonen/*Boot and Sons*.

The journey from Terneuzen to Delft took almost four hours, with them they carried a cash deposit of 1500 guilders, a small fortune. The van Aalst and Paulusse families had contributed what guilders they could. No wedding presents were given to the couple; instead a copper box was placed on a table at the reception centre, *'Cafe De Vriendschap'* where guests could drop in their guilders and cents, an arrangement that was so much more practical then receiving mainly, "useless cheap wedding presents", as Francine cheekily told me. Many families in Terneuzen pooled their resources for the collective good to start business or to purchase a house.

The Boot en Zonen Ship building yard at Delft had an excellent reputation for building iron ships that were *strong, fast, sleek, graceful sailing Klippers*, versatile and all-purpose cargo carriers suitable for the North Sea coastal waters and the shallow waterways of Europe. These river Klippers had speed, were cheap to operate, neither harming the environment nor polluting the waterways by using fuel, and they were propelled by the wind blowing in the sails that were made from locally grown hemp in Zealand Flanders. They were flat bottomed, an advantage for repairs and maintenance, and they could just be parked as it were on the mud flats near Terneuzen and set afloat again with high tides. For deep water coastal sailing they used adjustable side keels that would be lowered according to the wind force and water depth, giving the Klipper more stability and balance, ensuring it would not capsize. Kees and Francine 's ship when it was built had a length of 2800 m and a width of 569 m and could carry up to 174 tonnes of cargo.

The ship was registered in the home port of Terneuzen in Zealandic Flanders. This port was experiencing dynamic rapid industrial growth, several large Italian and French manufacturing and chemical works had settled there and the Belgians even built a large steel mill. Manufacturing required natural resources shipped from all the corners of the earth to Terneuzen, Gent or Antwerp. Zealandic Flanders farmers grew Flax, sugarbeets and large varieties of grains including forestry products like trees that needed transporting to the Bruynzeel pencil factory in North Holland. The future Paulusse's ship would have to be capable of transporting hundreds of tonnes of sugar beets for the Sugar Factories, or sand for the glass manufacturers, Rock Salt for the large Chemical Factories, heavy large rocks transported from Germany and Scandinavia for the fortification of the Zealand dykes, or sand and gravel extracted from the large sand banks in the river Scheldt. Here was a dynamic future.

The lives of Kees and Francine in Terneuzen always concerned themselves around the river Scheldt. To them it was like an orchestra of nature, clean flowing water with playful otters, seals and jumping fish, the Scheldt beat was to them the beat of life. Their work and bread were provided thanks to the commercial and natural riches and opportunities that the Scheldt offered and continued to offer. It shaped and formed their characters and personality, it made them understand the past like the 360 km long Scheldt stream that flowed into the future. The Scheldt culture was seen everywhere in sculpted art and architecture such as Scheldt Cothic, the many musical themes of Scheldt and in the Paintings of none other than *Peter Paul Rubens, Jan van Eyck, Pieter Bruegel,* and *Jan Gosseard.* Once Francine was a hostess for composer *Peter Benoit* who was on board the Belgian Royal Yacht *Prince Albert* when it visited Terneuzen. And even the poet *Jan Hammenecker* (1878-1932) had recited this poem at one of the birthday parties of the girls van Aalst:

> *"As long as I speak breathlessly with kidnapped language*
> *I will speak about you my Scheldt current."*

It was only natural that their ship was baptized *Scheldestroom* - a flow to the future.

Often large freighters that could not enter into the Terneuzen to Ghent Channel had to be partially unloaded into small river barges like the *Scheldestroom* so they could pass through the locks then unload in special warehouses for chemicals, calcium, iron ore, coal, wheat & grain storage. After much research the decision was made to place the order for the building of their ship, the *'Scheldestroom'*.

Smoking a large *Schimmelpennick cigar* Cornelis Boot greeted them with rare cordiality. He must have smelled their money, that being the reason why he was so amicable. His usual demeanour was one of a strict matter-of-fact business with a Calvinistic tone and manner not easily given to frivolity nor knowing the subtlety of diplomacy. Francine had changed all the hard silver and gold guilders for paper money tightly packed in her small fashionable leather handbag. Cornelis Boot was taken aback a little as it was rare that a Dutch woman would come along with her husband to place a ship-building order. The order was placed, and the 1500 guilders placed on the negotiating table as a down payment. The total cost of building the ship was 6500 guilders to be paid back over a five-year period at 4% interest, and a special insurance was signed just in case of an economic downturn when earnings would diminish. It would take four months to complete the building of the one mast river Klipper *Scheldestroom*.

After the contracts were signed Kees and Francine visited the nearby hennep growing fields cultivated by the manufacture of hemp products, which in those days was big business. *Hemp fibre was indispensable in the construction of sailing ships, as they could not sail without hennep rigging rope or hennep canvas.* It was also used for caulking material between the deck planks. No other natural fibre is as resistant to the forces of the open sea and the action of salt water. Waterproof gear for mariners was often made of hemp and the captain kept his log on hemp paper. Hemp oil lamps enabled the crew to read the Bible below deck. It, too, was printed on hemp paper. To survive shipwreck and ensure that food was on board, ships kept a supply of hemp seed. The large industrial hemp cultivation in the Netherlands had come to an end around 1915, apart from some smaller cultures for local use. The Golden Age of The Netherland would not have taken place without hennep.

In 1968 Kees told me that at times they smoked hennep mixed with pipe tobacco. No fuss was made. After all, most people were consuming a much harder drug, alcohol, he said, after discouraging his grandson never to indulge in smoking or in drinking to excess. In this case, he assured me that he never smoked much and rarely drank. I believed him because in that same year the two of us went on a two day cycle trip along the Zealandic Flanders water ways. Even at age 85 he was fast on the bike, while as a 19 year old I had difficulty keeping up with him!

The first baby girl was born early March 1911. For that birth Francine had gone to her mother's place to give birth to a baby daughter, Elisabeth Janna Paulusse. They called her little Bette, a healthy baby weighing 3.4 kg. I know this because Francine was present at the birth of my sister, Marianne, in 1961, and I can still hear her say, *"Oh how lovely! The same weight as little Bette!"* One of the reasons why Francine did not give birth on board was that Kees had landed a lucrative contract to transport bricks and needed extra deckhands on board to load and unload these bricks. Consequently there was no room for Francine and little Bette nor Leine who would help care for little Bette.

Starting in February to November 1911 the *Scheldestroom* plied the tidal rivers of the *Hollandsche IJssel* transporting bricks. Its shores were rich in river clay of different colours, brown, yellow, red, dredged from the river silt along all the major Dutch delta river systems. Many brick factories could be found along the shores of these rivers. The cargo manifest for 1911 shows that150 tonne peat to fuel the fire of the kilns was carried by the *Scheldestroom*.

On a very cold Saturday, the 16 December 1911, Francine gave birth to her second child, a son they named Jan-Pieter Paulusse who was born on board the *Scheldestroom*, delivered by a male midwife in the presence of a woman midwife. That day the *Scheldestroom* had been stranded on the sandbank just outside Terneuzen. This was not a disaster for flat bottomed ships, yet it was a bothersome situation. Francine, unexpectedly and too early, had felt the pangs of oncoming labour, then suddenly began her labour and she feared complications, so Kees got into his row boat and signalled a passing vessel to call the midwife when they reached the lock keeper. Within one hour two midwives had arrived, one male and one female, on a fast diesel emergency medical speed boat. The male midwives had training in obstetrics but the females not so much; they were good for easy births without complications. *Jan Pieter Paulusse* arrived without any complications. It was an easy birth, Francine told me, a piece of cake. His cradle was put under the Christmas tree in the warm cosy roof living quarters. Kees was rejoicing at the birth of a boy; he would be a future deckhand. In 1911, 60% of all babies were delivered by midwives at home and another 30% by male midwives at home, with only 10% in hospitals. Kees paid the male midwife six guilders and the female midwife 5 guilders. The diesel speed boat cost another 9 guilders - all paid in cash. Francine's sister Jane and her toddler Evert came down from Delft to stay for as long as it was needed, doing the cooking cleaning and spoiling the baby. Kees' older brother Ko came to help out as deckhand, a task previously done by Francine. Meanwhile, dark clouds were gathering; there was trouble brewing in the Balkans.

# CHAPTER 3

*The Great War 1914-1918*
*Skipper Kees was exempt from military service, the Scheldestroom*
*deemed essential and vital to the welfare of Netherlanders.*

Germany declared war on Tuesday, July 28. The Netherlands remained strictly neutral. The Netherlands mobilised and drafted over 200.000 young men into the military on Friday, July 31, 1914. On August 4, 1914, German troops crossed the border into Belgium; consequently, also conscripted were the two deckhands on the *Scheldestroom*. The removal of so many men from the workforce caused an immediate economic effect because The Netherlands economy depended on exporting produce and product and importing all of its natural resources including oil from the Netherlands East and West Indies. Therefore, the First World War caused a decline in domestic and international shipping, almost coming to a halt. Due to the lack of social security provisions, individual skippers ran into serious financial difficulties.

Kees and Francine were lucky they had paid off their final mortgage instalment owing on the *Scheldestroom* in June 1914. Twenty thousand Netherlands Army personnel were guarding the Netherland-Belgian borders in Zealandic Flanders alone. The influx of so many people caused a local economic boom to farmers and shippers such as the Paulusses. They say one man's loss is another man's gain, and that was true for many Netherlanders who profited from this war, a blessing in disguise. Many became wealthy selling food at inflated prices with few government controls. About the only thing was a workforce shortage. Skipper Kees was exempt from military service as he was the owner of an essential business vital to the welfare of Netherlanders. Still, it meant Kees and Francine sailed on their own without a crew. By now they had two children – Bette and Jan-Pieter, only three years old. Jane, Francine's unmarried sister from Delft and her young toddler Evert, had come down to stay and help Francine, with the children all neatly fitting into the tiny *Roef.* Crowded but *"Gezellig,"*/cosy said Francine. The competitive advantage was that the *Scheldestroom* did not use any petrol or diesel fuels in shortage. The raw forces of nature moved her 178 tonnes of cargo forward to anywhere. Elsewhere in The Netherlands food was rationed but not in Zealandic Flanders. Farmers there are easily the most efficient agricultural producers in the land. The *Scheldestroom* and its sister-ship the *Elizabeth* continued transporting potatoes, sugar beets, wheat, canola, barley and onions to the north of The Netherlands.

The German occupiers of Belgium needed sand and gravel, so they said, to repair war-damaged roads and houses. Again, for one month, the *Scheldestroom* carried sand and gravel pumped into her holds directly from the sandbanks outside the Terneuzen harbour. They had then sailed directly to *Zeebrugge* via the North Sea with the Germans and English giving assurances not to attack or confiscate ships flying the neutral Netherlands flag. Kees was sceptical; he did not trust either of the warmongering nations. The borders between Zealandic Flanders were permeable, almost informal, easy to cross; passports did not exist before 1920, and the free movement of people throughout Europe was the norm rather than the exception. By late 1914, after the fall of Antwerp, almost 250.000 Belgian refugees flooded into Zealandic Flanders and another 800.000 through the border provinces of Braband and Limburg. Francine remembered, "How chaotic it all seemed - all these frightened Belgian Refugees who were so much like us, they even spoke the Zealandic Flanders language and shared our cultural mindset, norms and values!"

I asked Opa Kees when I last spoke to him in 1968: How did the citizens mobilise for action all in a day when hundreds of people in Terneuzen volunteered to serve at the hastily set up *Hontenisse* refugee camp? He said it was not all that hard. Newspapers were printed three times a day: morning, afternoon and midday editions. There was no radio yet, but telephones and other electronic communications were adequate, and the telegram service quick and far-reaching. The Terneuzen Post office employed a lot of Telegram boys including Francine's younger brothers Piet and Hendrik. A state-of-the-art Post and Telegraphic Office installed the latest *Marconi Morse technology* serving ocean-going ships and inland shipping. Inland shipping skippers received telegrams about the arrival date and time when and where to expect large merchant cargo ships which were due to unload and reload into smaller vessels like the *Scheldestroom*. Even in those days messages to Netherlands East and West Indies, Australia, the USA or South Africa would only take a few minutes. He said that, besides these new electronic communications, people belonged to communities that were physically connected such as churches, sporting clubs, cultural societies, libraries, and - he said with a smile - the grapevine system. In a midsize harbour city like Terneuzen, nearly everybody knew each other, and every face was familiar. He pointed to groups of older men congregating around the canal locks and bridges, sitting on park benches in the shopping street, talking, greeting, chewing and spitting tobacco. School children passed on important messages to their parents. Many stay-at-home wives of Terneuzen gathered in small groups talking to their neighbours several times per day while scrubbing and re-washing their meticulously clean footpaths. There was a constant human face to face connection, real social media, unlike today, when millions feel isolated from the human touch, getting stressed and anxious, especially when they sit with bowed heads looking at their telephones as though it has all the answers. In that way we have degraded our interpersonal communications. So, in 1914 news travelled very quickly from mouth to mouth exhibiting the urgency of the messages through the emotions of the people. The van Aalst sisters and Hendrik, their youngest brother, volunteered to help organise the refugee camp at *Hontenisse* - not an easy task when it was raining, setting up tents in the mud, kitchens, sick bays, restrooms, storing food supplies. Many of the volunteers boarded the *Scheldestroom* at Terneuzen where it loaded donations from the citizenry - clothes, blankets, soap, water containers. The farmers pooled their resources together and chipped in one tonne of potatoes, as well as 600 kilos of assorted grains that the millers in Terneuzen ground into flour. Local bakers donated bread-making ingredients - yeast, sugar, salt - and the fire brigade loaned them their small water purification plant. Under a favourable wind, the *Scheldestroom* set sail to *Walsoorden*, the harbour of the municipality of Hontenisse. On board were four local Catholic priests and two Protestant ministers whose churches had been very liberal in collecting vital life-saving supplies, including medicines. The Terneuzen Hospital contributed medical supplies, two nurses and one doctor. It is worthwhile to note that all of these things were the initiatives of ordinary people. There was virtually no involvement by the Red Cross nor the Netherlands government because their function at that time was to care for military war casualties only and not civilian casualties. Refugees were not on the radar of the Red Cross of 1914.

All van Aalst sisters and young Hendrick were in high spirits on their way to Hontenisse singing patriotic and even Boer War songs as they went along encouraging others in their humanitarian tasks. One of the *Scheldestroom* cargo holds was converted into sleeping and resting quarters for all the van Aalst women and other volunteers while Francine, Kees and Jane and three children lived and slept in the *Roef*. A Terneuzen bicycle shop supplied the volunteers on the *Scheldestroom* with bicycles. Once they'd arrived at Walsoorden they'd all cycled merrily to the refugee camp together. Opa Kees said it might sound a bit frivolous, but it was essential to chill out and be cheerful, never forgetting there is always hope. At the camp, the van Aalst women sorted the refugees according to their means in three groups, the wealthy, middle class and the poor who had nothing but the clothes on their backs; the first two groups paid according to their means, while the third group did not have to pay.

Francine and all her sisters with other volunteers returned to Terneuzen rather quickly when they found that many of the refugees had caught typhoid fever, a severe bacterial infection spread by parasites. Yet the stream of refugees was unending, flooding the polder villages of Zealandic Flanders, not with water but with people. The local authorities quickly converted public buildings into emergency accommodation centres. Private accommodation suddenly stopped due to an outbreak of disease amongst the refugees. All refugees transferred to camps to contain the epidemic amongst the local population; by that time, the Netherlands Military had taken charge of the Refugee situation in a sustainable way, including the wearing of facemasks, and the frequent washing of hands in the many hand washing basins placed in the camp, filled with Lysol disinfectant. Twice daily hygiene inspection of the body and checking for lice in people's hair were methods to contain the Typhus pandemic. Crowding in the dormitories was forbidden. People kept a required distance until the Typhus pandemic passed. Here we can flash forward to 2020 and the Coronavirus., *CODVIC19* Is anything new under the sun?

A Note: Fast forward to the now 2020 Coronavirus lockdown. News doesn't travel any faster than it did in 1914 despite the internet and social media. Nowadays there seems to be a citizens' disconnect. Here is a test: Do you know your next-door neighbour? Chances are you don't, I mean, you don't scrub the footpaths together, do you? Would people today volunteer on a scale as they did in Terneuzen 1914 to help their fellows? Nowadays we spend much of our time in cyberspace. Even when I'm connecting to other people socially, I'm linking to them at a distance. I think this psychological distancing makes people feel disconnected but not if they have face-to-face time drinking coffee with people. In Western society, a significant proportion of time young adults are spending is not in actual face-to-face, but virtual reality.

Here in Australia the Government is spending millions of Australian Dollars in fighting loneliness and isolation in all ages' groups and sexes.

# CHAPTER 4



Winston Churchill, First Lord of the Admiralty, insisted that the first Royal Navy Brigade of 1500 men be stationed at Antwerp for possible defence. On October 17, 1914, the British lost Antwerp to a fierce enemy attack, the Germans taking control of this vital seaport. The defeated British had to flee to Zealandic Flanders where they crossed the Netherlands borders waiting for their internment. Many of these British men boarded the *Scheldestroom* for transport to Hontenisse because the roads were gridlocked by thousands of escaping Belgians and it being safer and quicker going by ship. The *Scheldestroom* cargo manifest shows a handsome profit was made; it needed to be so, covering the risks of losing ship and passengers, which were considerable, like hitting one of the hundreds of floating sea mines drifting loose in Antwerp harbour. The refugee camp also functioned as a temporary internment camp situated in the middle of large agrarian "Boer" polder communities. Tante/ *aunt* Leine, telling her story, felt sorry for them, "those English boys seemed so lost, bewildered and vacant, they couldn't believe that they had to surrender. But what turned out to be an irritation for the British was that Dutch farmers, like the South African farmers, did not like the English much. Memories of the recent Boer war were still raw, lingering on the cruelty inflicted upon the Boers in South Africa and the horrific internment of tens of thousands of Boer men and women and children of whom over 20.000 perished in the British concentration camps. No, I know he said you wouldn't read about it too much in history books, not even Netherlands books.

"Don't worry," said the Camp Commander to the British soldiers, *"we will not treat you the way you treated our Boer cousins in those horrible British and Australian-built concentration camps. Here in The Netherlands, we will treat you with respect and decency." The most popular songs in those days were the Boer war songs "My Sarie Marais", "Bobbejaan klim die berg".*

The Zealanders sang these patriotic songs everywhere they went. Yes, Kees said, Karma was no good for the First Royal Navy Brigade, although in the end, it panned out well for them. Many Zealanders said they would have probably been killed for nothing at the Somme like thousands of others. "Here with us, the lads are safe". The *Scheldestroom* was a fast sailing ship suitable to search for Belgian refugees that had unsuccessfully tried to escape their war-ravaged country on small unseaworthy boats. Skippers who had plied the treacherous waters of the *Honte estuary* entrance to the river Scheldt knew these waters like the backs of their hands and did not need sea pilots. At any rate, as soon as the Great War began the Netherlands closed the Scheldt to International shipping to maintain its neutrality.

Opa Kees frequently sailed via Vlissingen and Cadzand as far south to Ostend, Zeebrugge and Dunkirk, close to the North Sea coast, searching and rescuing drowning refugees.

Onboard the *Scheldestroom,* Netherlands Navy personnel took cognisance of the hideous mines the Germans and English were depositing along the Netherland coast. Constant danger and fear gripped the skippers that their ships would be sunk by a drifting mine or by German torpedoes or seized by the British, German and US navies. While picking up drowning refugees along the North Sea coast in Dutch waters along the Cadzand coast, a British Royal Navy fast minesweeper gave chase to the Scheldestroom. *"With no small amount of pride," Kees said, "we beat them on speed and manoeuvrability skills.* Luckily only four Belgians were on board and we were empty of cargo. This gave us a speed advantage and we knew where the treacherous sandbanks were, while the British did not; they needed pilots they didn't have." Francine took the steering wheel, and Kees set full sails catching the maximum winds, outracing the minesweeper, then suddenly an advection fog set in, a type of mist that forms from surface contact of horizontal winds; this fog can occur with windy conditions. "Thank goodness we lost the British as the noise of their engine faded away, the *Scheldestroom* vanished in the mist, and the English no longer saw our ship, slipping away into eerie silence," he laughed. "If I were a religious man I'd say the breath of God saved us from not being captured by the British Navy."

The Irony, of course, was that at the time there were thousands of British military personnel in the Netherlands internment camps being looked after like they were our children and yet the Brits kept confiscating our ships. Invariably there was a Netherlands outcry when the US government had in one night confiscated 200 Netherlands ships, all in one foul sweep, including large passenger liners such as the SS *Rijndam* and the most modern vessels in the Netherlands merchant fleet, amongst them the largest cargo ships in the World. All this went against the International Neutrality agreements. The Netherlands relationship with the US was fractious at any rate because ex-President Teddy Roosevelt had privately told Germany's Grand Admiral Alfred von Tirpitz and Kaiser Wilhelm to annex The Netherlands and incorporate it in the Greater German nation. Queen Wilhelmina got wind of it, and all hell broke loose.

## Cadzand Airplane Factory

One exciting pleasure, if there could indeed be pleasures in the war, was to see British, French and German Planes land on the beach at

Cadzand, situated only about 52 km from Flanders' battleground. More than frequently allied pilots would land deliberately or by mistake on Cadzand Beach just over the Belgian border. Kees couldn't remember how many planes he transported from Cadzand on the *Scheldestroom*, sailing them to Military bases in the North of The Netherlands. The military integrated all these different types of aircraft into the newly formed Netherlands Air Korps. The types of planes were a Bristol Type 22 - a British two-seater fighter - *a Fokker Eindecker*, a *Siemen-Schuckert* single-seat German fighter plane, and a French *Nieuport reconnaissance plane*. That is why the Netherlands Military called Cadzand Beach their "*Airplane Factory*". But the prize was the forced landing of a DeO/400, a long-range British bomber, which had accidentally bombed *Sluis, Sas van Gent, Goes, Vlissingen and Zierikzee* and accidentally fired on Netherlands ships mistaken for German ships.

*The British always denied that they accidentally bombed this and that, but in the end, they paid compensation. Still, it was all kept hushed. "Isn't a lot of history hushed or covered up, Opa?" I asked. He said, "Yes, of course, the Victors always write their version of history, in this case, the British."*

Oma/*grandmother* Francine remembered the conversation with the interned pilots. Were they deserters or was theirs an emergency landing? She answered, *"An emergency landing of course."* Silence, then audibly musing, *"Poor mothers of these young handsome, intelligent German and English boys and oh yes one was an Australian Pilot, but he had broken his leg."*

# CHAPTER 5



## The Great War had finished the birth of a skippers family

The explosion that catapulted the modern world on its course to dismantle itself was the Great War 1914 -18. It was called great on account of its size rather than for any notable merit. When its sequel broke out in 1941, the earlier conflict was renamed First World War in deference to the second.

The roaring twenties they called it, the age of feverish change, phenomenal wealth, decadence, loose women. The Dutch establishment was shocked by women having bobbed hair but not Francine she had always had bobbed hair as did all the van Aalst girls they were well ahead of the pack. Yet their lives were not frenzied by the whirlwinds governing the Dancebands music setting the rhythm of the 1920s known as the antebellum, the between war years. It was an era where Americanisms were infiltrating Dutch culture and could cause an identity crisis much to the chagrin of the Churches and the ruling conservative Government. However, Kees and Francine were too busy procreating a family of boys it seemed.

The sun shone brightly on a cloudless perfect day on the last Tuesday in the month, September 30, 1924. Skipper Cornelis Paulusse, my grandfather, called Kees for short, hurried excitedly and with great strides, his black wooden shoes clattering on the cobbled stones. Making his way to the Terneuzen Stadhuis/ town hall to record the birth of his and young wife Francine's fourth child and second son. Het Stad Huis (Dutch for town hall) was the place to register births and deaths. The Paulusses' annals show that they had been making this journey over the cobbled stones since 1594. The town hall was built after Prince William of Orange granted city rights. 'What's your new son's name?' Mijnheer (Mr) Huizinga, the registrar, asked Kees. 'His name is Pieter Paulusse, we will call him Piet.' Thereupon, Kees' signature was placed as the informant. As the custom was all the menfolk at Het Stad Huis received a large Dutch cigar, congratulations were said. The women employees received Belgian chocolates that Kees had purchased cheaply in Ghent two days ago when he had to deliver 200 tonnes of sand at a glass factory. He was going to sail there again in a couple of hours as soon as the felicitations were over. Kees was well known for his humanitarian aid during World War I when Nederland was neutral, and Belgium was invaded. He sailed his sailing river clipper ship De Scheldestroom laden with food and medicine to relieve the impoverishment of the war-ravaged Belgian population. Everyone knew that the Germans and the English were shooting at his ship. Yet Scheldestroom sailed through it all. They called it the miracle ship, and the devout Catholic Belgians saw the hand of God over this good ship.

The Stadhuis women employees wanted to know how Kees and Francine were going to cope with an extra child as living space on the Scheldestroom was limited. It had just one small cabin, serving as a living and sleeping quarters for two adults and now, with the birth of Piet, four children. Kees told them that they managed through utilizing every small space. Piet's baby cot was the hull of a yet unfinished Tjalk model ship which Kees was in the process of building for Queen Wilhelmina. It was destined that Piet's entire childhood was to be spent on the Scheldestroom.

Several years hence on a cold and windy Thursday the date being November 17, 1926. Rugged up early in the very cold morning, Kees repeated his walk to the Stadhuis again his wooden skipper clogs clattering and echoing over the cobblestones.

Hurried on his way to register the birth of his third son Cornelis Paulusse named after himself, they called him Kees. Who for a long time was called "Kleine Kees" meaning little Kees so as not to confuse the two Keeses. Again Kees gave every male administrator a large, expensive Dutch cigar. Francine had purchased three boxes of fresh creamy Belgian chocolates in Antwerp, and these were given to the women administrators who worked there. There was another reason for his generosity that paid to be in the Stahuis's good books. Stadhuis employees also issued a variety of licenses for this that and the other. They collected council taxes for marine services rendered to shipping; so Kees's gifts weren't bribery but tools for subtle relationship building.

Yet again, on Thursday, June 28 1928, Kees made his way to the Terneuzen Stadhuis. Registring, the birth of Abraham Paulusse, his fourth son, endearingly called Bram, again the cigars were lit and the Belgian chocolates passed around. This time Kees was in a hurry as the Scheldestroom was leaving port within one hour, laden with tonnes of potatoes, onions and peas destined for Amsterdam. Extra food was needed for athletes and visitors of the IX Olympic Games in Amsterdam scheduled to commence on July 28 1928. He was not half proud to mention the Scheldestroom with other sailing klippers delivered millions of locally baked bricks. Used for the Amsterdam Art Deco Olympic Stadium. The Art Deco Olympic Flame tower overlooking the stadium was also made of bricks, significant because Amsterdam gave birth to the modern Olympic flame lighting ceremony.

It is interesting to note here that during the 1914-1918 war period, no Paulusse children were born. Francine said this was a deliberate act of family planning, she thought it not wise to bare children. Especially when the nation could either be invaded by England, Germany or France. She was wary after seeing the miserable state of refugees who carried babies and young children. No good bringing babies into the world of neutral Nederland, threatened continuously by a war emergency. Besides the Scheldestroom could hit a mine or be confiscated by warmongers like Germany, England or France. They had sought experts advice and read about "stopping" and the other on the "spacing" of births from a Dr Rutgers, an emerging Dutch expert in the field of family planning.

When Bram was born, their oldest daughter Bette was already 17 years old. She was working as a housekeeper with a rich widower in Gent. The eldest son Jan-Pieter was 16 and was an apprentice mechanic living onshore boarding at the house of his future wife Bets van der Hooft. Jana, the second eldest girl, had just turned 15 and looked after her elderly grandparents Opa and Oma van Aalst. This growth of the family was spaced because the Roef living quarter on the Scheldestroom would not have been able to fit all of the six children plus two parents all at once. As soon as Piet was five years old he moved to 'het Voor onder', a little space created near the bow of the ship were spare sails and ropes were kept. Kees had lined the steel plates with insulating material then covering it with wood veneer sheets to keep out the freezing temperatures in the wintertime. Spaces were created for three beds, later all of the three boys used this space as their bedroom.

I had often wondered about personal hygiene in such small spaces. One day I asked Francine about it she said everyone living on board had to wash their whole bodies, including hair. There was a little washing closet the size of a small shower cubicle with a deep water basin, warm water was supplied by an electric water pump. In winter the water was kept warm with a heating element that Kees had placed in the small freshwater tank. In the summer months, the men would just jump over board in the crystal clear waters. Most of the channels at that time were not polluted with chemicals, oils and plastic. One could still lather up with soap as the water was not as harsh as most of the Zeeland fresh waterways did not have a high concentration of calcium and magnesium ions.

It was necessary to wash oneself every day because the Scheldestroom sometimes carried cargo that was not clean. Such as mud-dust from potatoes and sugar beets or coal grime seeping out of the coal filled hessian bags. None of the family would enter the roef with work clothes and unwashed. Francine was always proud that she had the first electric washing machine in Zealandic Flanders. Made by Kees of course who put an electric motor on her hand turned washing tub, people came to view it from far and near. Actually, Kees had got the idea when he saw an electric washing machine at the Paris world fair in 1900.

Francine and Kees homeschooled all their children with the help of a homeschool syllabus designed for skipper's children consisting of exercise books emphasizing the three R's reading writing and arithmetic. These syllabuses were in line with every school in the land. When they were waiting for cargo, the children would attend the local school. However, after primary school, the boys studied at technical colleges. They stayed with Bette or Janna or with aunties or uncles, who were by then living or working onshore.

"Optimistic Tenacity, Originality and Creativity" should have been the family motto. This is not to say that there were never any besetting problems every family usually has some cross to bear of one thing or another. Kees's older brother Abraham, we kids called him oom Bram also had a sailing klipper. It was a few tonnages more heavier than the Scheldestroom, and it had two masts it was named "Elizabeth" after their mother.

The Scheldestroom and the Elizabeth were an item, so to speak. The brothers Paulusse looked out for each other's business and their health and welfare. Cargo would often be shared between the two ships, they'd work and sail in tandem as one unit. Bram was never married probably because his mother made him promise to care for his younger brother Jan who suffered a disability. As a young child oom, Jan would chase and tease me in a strange but friendly way not always appreciated by me. Often when I met him on the street chewing tobacco, he would ask me if I wanted something of course as a child I'd shake my head indicating yes. I'm Jan would then place the chewing tobacco in my hand much to my horror. Later Francine explained that he had a sense of juvenile behaviour and not to take oom Jan too serious. Now, after having studied psychology, I'm almost sure he was somewhere on the spectrum of autism, and he clearly suffered from bipolar. Not that he was diagnosed as such but having met him as a very young child and as psychology student I would see thing Jan had drawn and written. I well recall his dramatic, almost uncontrolled tantrums. I was surprised though that he had never fallen overboard and drowned he could not swim. For thirty years he was a deckhand on the Elizabeth, but they had to hire a minder for him. He was never seen as a burden by the family except that everyone felt sorry for Bram in not having a wife and family may be on account of Jan. The Elizabeth was later confiscated or stolen by the Germans without compensation, but I will leave that for later.

They called it the roaring 1920s when the Netherlands experienced exponential economic growth that benefited the Scheldestroom. Home comforts such as washing machines, refrigerators, vacuum cleaners and radios were all made by Dutch-owned Phillips Electronics. Other products such as the Spijker cars were popular with thousands of the nouveau riche who had earned their fortune in the black market during World War 1. The growing economy created a feeling of optimism about the future. He also recognized that many areas in The Netherlands's were not sharing in the economic dividends.

The circumstance of the Paulusse's and their Scheldestroom was right, they had no debt. However, Skippers whose boats were to too small and had a hard time competing for freight. The Scheldestroom was lucky there was a lot of work for this type of sailing ship because motor fuel and coal were still rationed and Kees competed on price and speed. Talent, initiative and creativity are abundant in the Paulusse family. Demonstrated when Kees's friend Loe Boone a garage owner gave him an old Ford T model engine. Kees completely overhauled the engine by himself and placed it in his large rowing boat, converting it into a push and pull mini tug. Using opportunity and foresight saved a lot of money that they would otherwise have to pay for tug boats needed to move the Schelde stroom through the many channel locks. Thank goodness Francine, and the girls no longer had to pull the Scheldestroom by hand along some of the very narrow channels where they could not safely sail or if there was no wind. They made money also by provided mini tug services to other sailing clippers.

The Schelde stroom had always been in the "Wilde Vaart" meaning unregulated cargo shipping of all sorts. It was competitive and more profitable because there was no need for a middleman, thus saving much money. The only drawback was one had to socialize and negotiate over a Dutch gin or beer with customers directly in designated freight cafes. On occasions, Kees would come home slightly drunk, and Francine did not like she was fearful he would fall off the gangway plank and drown. Kees with his brother Bram maintained valuable networks of relationships with friends acquaintances. Vital ingredients in the world of shipping and cargo handling these networks enabled them to run their business to function effectively. Today I would say they had invaluable social capital. A shipping family such as the hospitable Paulusses inevitably made friends in every port. There were always streams of exciting visitors, friends and foes alike coming on board De Scheldestroom for coffee and gezelligheid.

1920scwere a bonanza for the Paulusses en every way.

Healthy children were born prosperity, and new technology was king. Yet, the excellent time crashed in 1929, beginning with the crash of the New York Stock Exchange; the consequences reverberated all over the world, including the Netherlands

# CHAPTER 6

*The Great Depression*
*"they were survivalist by nature and not easily daunted by an adversary"*

The difficulties for Kees and Francine began in 1931 when there was not much freight; the economic depression had set in. The *Scheldestroom*'s last few cargoes were 400 tons of potatoes to be dumped in the North Sea by order of the Dutch Government. "The fish will be happy," Kees wrote on a postcard sent from Scheveningen.

They were absolutely disgusted by the gross ineptitude of Dutch Prime Minister Hendrik Colijn and his conservative right-wing party. Hundreds of thousands of Nederlanders went to bed hungry, not being able to feed their families properly on the meagre state welfare sustenance they received. The authorities ordered all plant foods to be destroyed, as many people had no jobs and no money to buy anything, let alone food. All this created a climate of gloomy pessimism, discouragement and bitterness amongst unemployed Netherlanders. It was an anxious time for many.

The Paulusses did as much as they could and smuggled potatoes to designated secret warehouses. Their children Jan-Pieter, Bette and Janna filled up large hessian bags full of spuds, secreting them away on the *Scheldestroom* and on its sister ship, *Elizabeth*. Kees manufactured a potato grating machine to turn some of these into dried powder for baking bread. All the van Aalst sisters would come on board and help with the bottling of vegetables and fruits such as beans, peas, beetroot and carrots. They rescued the vegetables so to speak from wanton immoral destruction by the state. Some of this food they ate themselves, but most of it was redirected and distributed by the van Aalst sisters to the unemployed people of Terneuzen. They'd observed the dreadful shenanigans of politicians. They couldn't believe Parliament, a coalition of Christian parties, agreeing to dump hundreds of tonnes of vegetables. Unbelievable, and it had not helped a soul, only causing incalculable misery. "Jesus must have wept," Kees said with a wink. The approach of Francine's distant cousin, the brilliant *Paul van Zeeland*, Prime Minister of Belgium, was much better in managing the economic depression and guaranteed 4% interest on savings and froze all prices and forbade the destruction of much-needed food. Then Francine belted the Netherlands Prime Minister *Hendrik Colijn* and his inept henchmen. The crisis intensified, and there was no more freightage, and the shipping of cargo almost stopped. Exports reduced, diminishing agriculture and manufacturing production, resulting in thousands of skippers being laid up or worse still, ruined. These were primarily those sailing on the Rhine to and from Germany. The *Scheldestroom* was laid up voluntarily by Kees himself, and its use was diverted to a type of floating shipwright maintenance centre.

At this time his first son, Jan-Pieter Paulusse, had started an automotive repair business in Terneuzen, made possible with financial help from Kees and Francine. Jan-Pieter's garage specialised in replacing old engines for new and Kees would help him in reconditioning these old motors. They say necessity is the mother of invention, and this was undoubtedly true in Paulusse's case.

The *Scheldestroom* cargo hold was soon changed into a small boat-building centre. In this place, Kees converted ordinary rowing boats or sloops into motorised push and pull boats, placing the engines he himself had refurbished into these boats. One such order came from the well-to-do *Vermast family* in Terneuzen, converting their large utility rowboat into a sizeable sailing yacht. This job alone took 6 months to complete, even employing other men. Daughters Jana and Bette and their young brothers were apprenticed to sand, paint and remove rust from decks and hulls. There were no gender-specific roles on the *Scheldestroom* other than those of childbirth.

A sloop conversion is finished and we see the little yacht *De Zwerver* being lifted out of the hull of the Scheldestroom.The woman pulling the rope is Jana their second daughter.

Kees' cache of talents and ingenuity bore fruit, while his reputation of also being a master vintage model shipwright grew as his models sold to museums, kings and queens. I found a 1960 newspaper article in a Dutch daily *'Het Vrije Volk'.*/ *The Free People*. Here is the translation and picture of the item:

> *"Old skipper Paulusse from Terneuzen cannot forget ship*
> *life. His love for the sea and his crafting talents were*
> *significantly well expressed when many years ago he made a*
> *crib for his son. The Oakwood-made baby cradle naturally*
> *took on the shape of a curved, slender sailing ship. Later,*

*says Mr Paulusse, 'when my son outgrew the cradle, I placed a deck in the frame and further rigged it into a sailing ship model. I used the model to teach my sons and daughters the art of sailing.' The 80-year-old skipper, once in the unregulated ship cargo business, still finds his daily activities amid his many vintage sailing models. He reckons that models of all the boats he made throughout his life would not fit into his big living room. 'I've been involved with this hobby since I was sixteen. You can imagine that I must have made quite a few'. There is an enormous deal of interest in the miniature sailing ships of the former skipper from Terneuzen. He has regular customers throughout the Netherlands, and they are happy to pay four to five hundred guilders per ship. It takes him seven weeks every day for ten hours working in his narrow utility room that he has set up as a studio. Skipper Paulusse's collection included a lot of showpieces. He built Princess Beatrix's Green Draeck and made a ship for a marriage present to Queen Fabiola and King Baudouin of Belgium. Alas, we were unable to admire them. 'As soon as I complete a boat it is sold, another buyer knocks on the door.' Laughingly he says, 'My products just fly away. Anyway, you can see for yourself, I was never able to keep one for myself.'"*

I clearly recall the family conversations we had about the "Great Depression", as we called it in Australia. The hundreds of thousands of unemployed Netherlanders in the mid-1930s led to a dire and hopeless existence for those affected by the world's economic malaise. The images created by the media of these crisis years are often of a gloomy and dreary decade. Unemployment, regrettably the status of too large a minority. On the other hand, however, the majority did have a job, and they were not necessarily worse off than before. No Government handouts for skippers like Kees and Bram was provided; fortunately, they were survivalist by nature and not easily daunted by an adversary. To bring more cheer into their lives, they purchased a Phillips Point

Radio, an art deco beauty made from beautiful wood. I still have it in my possession today, and it has a story all its own for later telling, and yes it still works! During the depression, many songs were sung to lift the mood and spirits like *"Happy days are here again"*. Kees's favourite music with an utterly uplifting catchy tune of the time was, *"Be a smiling sun, a happy face, love comes to those who do good"*.

For the umpteenth time, Francine told me to focus on the bright side of life. *"Whatever gets your attention gets you."* She would emphasise success stories of the 1930s such as the triumph of the KLM's *Uiver* taking part in the legendary London to Melbourne race. Dubbed as the 'World's Greatest Air Race', leaving London in October 1934, 21 planes competing to fly halfway around the world in the quickest time. The KLM crew was successful: the *Uiver* landed second in Melbourne after more than ninety hours. It took first place in the handicap, making an emergency landing at Albury, and its citizens pulled it out of the mud. *Kees said that the Uiver's achievements symbolised the modernising of the country.* The Netherlands became a world leader in aviation, manufacturing Fokker aeroplanes with KLM, created the world's first modern international airline. KLM and Fokker worked together as a team funded by the Dutch people and led by investor Queen Wilhelmina. The Paulusses with thousands of others had invested 100 guilders in getting Fokker and KLM off the ground, so to speak. Oh yes, Francine also mentioned the breakthrough of the bicycle as a popular means of transport. At the end of the 1930s, the Dutch rode on approximately 3.5 million bikes in a population of 8 million people.

During this period of economic crisis and later during the Second World War there were rarely any shortages of food on the *Scheldestroom*. Francine had a golden string to her bow: she was a fantastic cook. Consequently, I called her "Oma Chef". Nothing was packet food or manufactured food; at that time fridges were not the norm onboard, so all the meat was smoked or put into huge stone pots. The fried cutlets and bacon, preserved in their own fat, kept for months. She would make sauerkraut from cabbage and salt. It took weeks to cure before sizeable portions would be distributed to neighbours, friends and family. Bottling fruits and vegetables in times of plenty was an activity that all the van Aalst sisters helped in. Cleaning and 'blanching' vegetables before bottling cleanses the surface of dirt and organisms, as well as brightening the colour and stopping the leakage of vitamins. Francine baked all her own varieties of bread in the little oven Kees had made himself. He had made a special metal pipe which looked like a hollow needle which was gently forced through the threads of the hessian bags. The sugar flowed through this metal stash pipe into a container. The same was done for grains, molasses and peas; this was of course food that was destined to be dumped whilst many went hungry.

In 1959 whilst Tante Leine and Oma Francine were doing bottling in their small kitchen at home in Dahlia straat 7, Terneuzen, I turned the conversation to things they'd worried about during the crisis years. Did they ever worry? They burst out laughing. "Sure!", they said, but explained it was more of a healthy, managed stress rather than a nagging, constant, worrying feeling. Stress, they reckoned, wasn't a bad thing, as it helped them get up in the morning. "I suppose," said Oma, "I was more concerned, instead of being stressed, about something that affected the wellbeing of my children and Kees.

*We worked at feeling safe and secure despite all of us living in a floating tub so to speak, that if not managed right could sink," she said with a wink. "Sailing the Scheldestroom in rough seas, waves thundering, smashing all over the creaking deck hatches, everything shaking, and seeing poor Kees struggling to adjust the sails, getting soaking wet, me on the rudder wheel, the kids by themselves in the Roef, unperturbed, playing with puzzles or doing board games. There simply was no time for stress, anxiety or worry.*

We knew how to handle the sea, and our ship was always in a seaworthy shape. The kids were trained for a maritime emergency, but they understood their safety was still first and foremost. They could all swim virtually from the time they were born, and safety drills and First Aid training soon followed after swimming lessons. Yes," Francine continued, "economic crises were like lousy weather. Still, in the end, we'd eventually get over it, nothing lasts forever. See how Kees and my boys and girls coped and thrived during adversity? Oh, they had such resilience! I'm not ashamed to be a proud mother," She smiled.

Tante Leine confirmed, "Yes, same with my kids. They were surviving and thriving. Until our ship was bombed by the 'moffen' [a Dutch derogatory name for wartime Germans]. But," Leine continued, "I have to let out a secret about the children swimming as babies. *Your Oma had never been able to swim herself in all those forty years of living on the Scheldestroom!* Her safety was ensured by several strategically placed life-saving buoys at hand for Francine just in case she'd fall into the water." Francine smilingly said that she was never that drunk to fall into the water - laughter all round - because she had been a teetotaller throughout her married life. Opa Kees, who had been working on one of his ships' models nearby, silently listening, agreed that so many of his contemporaries had agonised themselves literally to death without taking action. "Adversity is something we can overcome, whereas a mental disorder is something to be managed as we did with my brother Jan and his mental problems. *Don't worry, be happy!* he said, years before the song with these words was made famous.

*The depression years were not bad years for families who had trained survival instincts, those that could think outside the square and that dared to try something different and had the kind of living skills that one did not learn at a University or at school.* Francine and Kees stipulated the value of thrift, recycling, making and manufacturing things, but not at the price of sacrificing generosity toward one's fellows. Their own example and practice of forbearance in extraordinarily tough economic times emphasised self-reliance, teaching their kids survival skills, predominately how to prosper during this crisis. In one of his letters to me, Opa Kees mentioned that these skill-sets on surviving are not taught at school or University. And with a touch of humour he said they don't teach boys to spin their own wool and knit socks. Well my boys can," he added. Who needs wool and knitting mills when you can turn at home? The textile and woollen mills had nearly all shut in The Netherlands, throwing some 20,000 textile workers onto the unemployment heap and onto the streets.

Francine, as any forward-looking responsible mother in 1932 would do, opened savings accounts for each child. In my shoebox of kept memories, I found the bank books of the savings accounts of the Paulusse children, my aunties and uncles. They delighted in depositing their loot. Both Piet and his brother, Kees, smiling, indicating a certain amount of pride in their achievements and ability to earn money, deposited four to five, and sometimes ten guilders every month into their savings accounts. They achieved this as eleven-year-old boys who, with their older sister Janna, collected old newspapers. Soaking, pressing and drying, rolling them into balls, selling them as heating balls, cheaper than coal. "Longer lasting" was their marketing and sales motto. Sometimes people were poor and had no money so they would then barter for goods or services in exchange.

On the *Scheldestroom,* the talk had changed from the economy to marriage, three marriages that would soon be celebrated. The sewing machines and the knitting needles aboard the *Scheldestroom* were kept busy. Weddings were planned for the years 1938 and 1939. Women were sewing, making dresses, the boys knitting their own woollen socks. Francine sewing a long orange pennant to be flown atop the *Scheldestroom* mast together with the red, white and blue Dutch tricolour to celebrate the marriage of Crown Princess Juliana with the German Prince Bernhard on a cold Thursday, 7 January 1937. Their firstborn son, Jan-Pieter, was married to Elizabeth van der Hooft on Thursday, 13 October 1938. Janna, their second daughter, soon followed by marrying her longtime sweetheart, Adriaan de Zeeuw in 1939. Kees and Francine paid for both wedding receptions at Cafe De Vriendschap. They had done well in the depression but no thanks to the government, no, they had always sailed their own ship through stormy seas into calm waters.

Francine parents *Jana and Jan van Aalst* celebrating their 50 wedding anniversary 1936 at Java Straat 32 among their grandchildren. Five of Francine and Kees' children are here including three of Leine's children. *Corry Bootgezel Doeselaar* a daughter of Sophia van Aalst who died too young she the smiling girl in the middle she migrated to Australia in 1952.

# CHAPTER 7



Hitler had attacked Poland in 1939, and Kees' intuitive feelings predicted that it wouldn't be long before Nazi Germany would invade the Netherlands. I always thought that being intuitive was a gift from the gods as it takes courage to follow intuition. As it was before the First World War, this time again, the government mobilised all men over 18 years. Consequently, the Scheldestroom lost its deckhand to the military.

At the time, my father, Piet, just 15 years old, was working on a Belgian oil tanker named *Nijverheid*. This ship was captained by his uncle, *Gerit Tanis*, who was married to Marie, the youngest of the van Aalst sisters. They, too, lived on their boat and Piet boarded with them. The oil tanker *Nijverheid* was designated as a vital oil transporter by the Belgian government. They placed defence guards on the *Nijverheid*; consequently, Piet returned to work with his father on the Scheldestroom.

Up to a point, these were idyllic times, an uneasy calm before the storm creating an ominous feeling amongst the populace. The ancient River Scheldt, always stunning and even more beautiful than in reality, the streaming freshwater, yet unpolluted, containing a lot of fish, especially eels ready to catch. Graceful sailing klippers, alluring to behold in full sail with their swords and brown tanned sails skillfully navigating in all kinds of weather, powerfully zig-zagging against the wind. Fresh, clean drinking water was pumped directly out of freshwater channels without any filtering, and nobody got sick because of drinking the fresh fast-flowing waters of the Scheldt. 1940 was different to 2020; the water now is unfit to consume. Piet and his younger brothers got up early in the summer to wash the dew off the shutters; it is terrible for the tar they said. Still, I think that's just an excuse for getting them out of bed early; teenage boys are notorious for not being early risers.

A few days after the war broke out on May 10, 1940, the Scheldestroom lay ready to sail, loaded up with large, massive trees in *Walsoorden* destined for the Bruynzeel pencil factory in *Zaandam* near Amsterdam. A good sailing breeze blew that afternoon, sped them across the Western Scheldt unusually fast. As the Scheldestroom neared the little harbour port of *Hansweert*, suddenly and without warning they witnessed their first bombardment of the Second World War. The Luftwaffe's Stuka "dive bomber" with their *kriegspiel /war games,* of horrific screaming sirens attached to wings deliberately terrorising the population and weakening the morale of their enemy. Causing mass fear through deafening howls as the Luftwaffe dropped their bombs on the channel locks at *Hansweert*, luckily they fell far away from the oncoming Scheldestroom. Immediately, as a precaution, Francine hid her young boys, Kees and Bram, under the heavy, thick, wooden, teak table. Kees and son Piet, rapidly manoeuvred the Scheldestroom around back towards *Walsoorden*. When they returned to *Walsoorden harbour*, they could 'not believe what they saw. *"A frightening shemozzle of disarray,"* said Francine. She felt compassion for these Belgian and French troops so poorly and pitifully equipped. In old-fashioned equipment still pulled by horses and dog wagons, troops were escaping in a state of disorganised panic. Fortunately, Kees and Francien kept all their senses together. The French commander ordered the Scheldestroom to block the port of Walsoorden, preventing the Germans from landing. Inevitably ordering Kees to anchor the Scheldestroom in the middle of the port, there the French would dynamite the ship, blowing it up. But quick thinking and smart Kees said in French, *"Monsieur tu vois mon bateau est bordé de grands arbres il ne peut pas couler,"* which, translated, means, *'Sir, you can see that my ship, loaded with big massive trees, will never sink."*

"Yes, that could be the case," answered the French commander. Suddenly in a flash, diving at full throttle with screaming sirens two Luftwaffe Stukas finished their conversation. Within seconds the French and Belgian troops evaporated, fleeing without blowing up the Scheldestroom.

Eight months before the German invasion of the Netherlands, Jan - Pieter, Kees' and Francien's eldest son, who was married to Elisabeth van der Hooft, was mobilised in October 1939, to serve in the Dutch Navy. On Wednesday, May 15, 1940, the day the Netherlands surrendered (but not Zeeland) it fought on, together with the British Navy and 60.000 French and Belgian troops still fighting in Zeeland. At that time Jan-Pieter served on a Dutch Navy minesweeper; it was a converted fishing trawler, clearing mines on the Scheldt river regularly dropped by the Luftwaffe. Around 2 pm on that fateful Wednesday, four Luftwaffe Stukas dive-bombed and sprayed the Dutch Navy ship with gunfire, seriously injuring Jan-Pieter, hit by shrapnel in the abdomen. The Luftwaffe planes returned to finish their bombing mission. As luck would have it, the nearby British escort destroyers, *HMS Whitley* and *HMS Valentine* opened up their anti-aircraft artillery. This action by the British saved the lives of the Dutch sailors. Unfortunately, at 2.30 pm, the HMS Valentine copped the two bombs meant for the Dutch minesweeper. The Valentine's captain beached his ship in a sinking condition on a dyke near Terneuzen, lamentably killing 31 of Valentine's crew and injuring a further 21. With much anguish of heart, Francine, showing the tears of a mother's love, said that they lost their dear Jan-Pieter in January 1941, due to shrapnel infections and a lack of medical care. RIP oom/*uncle* Jan.

Things soon started to deteriorate after the British navy along with Belgian and French troops retreated. I recently found an old newspaper in which Kees was interviewed by *"Het Vrije Volk"*, a major Dutch media outlet. Concerning the attempted impounding of the Scheldestroom for conversion to a landing craft used for invading England:

*"In 1940, after having unloaded trees in Rotterdam, Paulusse arrived back in Terneuzen, when the Germans ordered him to return to Rotterdam immediately. The Nazis had a tugboat at the ready to tow the Scheldestroom back to Rotterdam. Paulusse promised a group of forlorn-looking Belgian skippers who lost their ships to the Nazis, 'If I can keep my boat I will bring you home for free.' The Germans did not find the Scheldestroom suitable for sailing to England. So Paulusse could redeem his promise, and he got the duped seven Belgian families with all their worldly goods and chattels to their shore addresses."*

The Nazis, being victorious in Europe, and the Netherlanders, including their economy, settled down almost as usual under occupation. That economic security lull would soon change. Kees said that everybody, men, women, beast, machinery and commerce, even the whole of the Dutch government bureaucracy, worked for the Germans, including the Scheldestroom; there was no choice. However, restrictions soon came: listening to the radio was forbidden. The German Nazis confiscated radios, bicycles, food, copper and bronze without payments or compensation. The occupiers introduced ration cards acting as a currency against the emerging and profitable black market. Time and again the Scheldestroom and all Dutch ships remained targets by RAF fighter planes interrupting and destroying German supply lines and miraculously killing no one on the Scheldestroom except for shrapnel-damaging decks and hatches. Still, no lives were lost - such a lucky ship.

The Germans continuously cleared the magnetic sea mines in the Scheldt after being dropped by the RAF. Come what may Francine kept worrying about her van Aalst sisters Leine and Marie, both married to skippers. Her concerns weren't unfounded as a tragedy soon struck. Leine's husband, Bram, while sailing his ship during a dog fight between the Luftwaffe and the RAF in the sky over his boat, was killed by shrapnel, leaving behind three girls and their mother.

During the five-year duration of the war, food became scarce. The Germans destined Zealandic Flanders farm produce for themselves at the expense of Dutch citizens. Kees illegally stole some of this produce, surreptitiously giving it away to the Dutch underground for distribution to Nederlanders. The unloading of food supplies was always done under the watchful eyes of an NSBer (*Nationaal-Socialistische Beweging*) the much-hated pseudo police force collaborating with the enemy. My dad, Piet unloading potatoes in Rotterdam, was known to deliberately manipulate the ships' loading boom into shaking, causing a fair amount of potatoes to spill over onto the Scheldestroom's gangway. He'd yell to the kids to right away come onboard to gather the spilt potatoes, and within nanoseconds, on one occasion about twenty kids jumped on board, helping themselves. The collaborator jumped on board the ship and ordered the kids off the boat. Piet destained and browbeat *"the dirty"* NSBer off the Scheldestroom, simultaneously urging the kids to run whilst playing for time arguing with the NSB'er, who immediately alerted the Gestapo officers, and within 30 minutes they took Piet to the Nazi Sicherheitspolizei (*Security Police*) in Rotterdam. Kees arrived back 30 minutes later after he'd secured new cargo and drawn up a freight manifest. Francine, upset about the drama with the NSBer, urged Kees to go and speak to the chief of Gestapo. Kees knew this German from a previous meeting in Rotterdam when the Germans wanted to confiscate and impound ships including the Scheldestroom. Kees used his best psychology because he knew how easily bruised egos drive fanatics and fascists, and they like to feel superior. He wasted no time in making Piet apologise to the NSBer and telling the Gestapo chief that his 16-year-old son had a mental condition, promising he would discipline him severely. Kees understood the narcissist nature of fascists and knew how to stroke the egos of the NSBer and Gestapo types. He again apologised, releasing Piet without further ado. Much relieved, they returned to the Scheldestroom. Kees, of course, explained to Piet that all this acting performance was just a front. Had he not performed that way it would have meant a stint in a Nazi rehabilitation camp in Vucht.

Back in Terneuzen the Scheldestroom laying alongside the marina when Kees heard the shouting and commandeering of the Gestapo he yelled out to 'Grandy', as in 'grandmother', which is what he called his wife to us children. "The Krauts are already on the SchepenDijk/*Ship's Dyke* with a few trucks taking everything that's fast and loose, stealing all things made of copper and brass.

*Tell the boys to throw the Scheldestroom's large bronze ship's bell overboard and also the Philips point radio; the Gestapo is doing finicky searches. The boys, Kees, Piet and Bram, can dive and retrieve them later."*

It is worth noting that the radio was placed in a secret place in the Roef/ *deckhouse*, together with a waxed hessian bag with two heavy bricks. Five minutes before the Gestapo invaded the Scheldestroom doing razzias, the little Philips point radio was slid in the bag and pushed silently into the water. It sank instantly to the bottom of the channel. A very small fishing float would indicate the position of items, including the Scheldestroom bell, also thrown overboard. As soon as it became safe, the boys would dive and retrieve the *Art Deco Philips point radio* which I still have, and it plays even after 90 years. They used to make things to last before a consumer-driven economy that introduced inbuilt obsolescence.

Early in 1942, daughter-in-law Bets, still grieving for the passing of her husband Jan- Pieter, asked Kees and Francine to help hide three Jewish people - a mother and two boys - on the Scheldestroom. She realised that during the economic depression, Kees constructed a secret space to store food saved from shameful destruction by the Dutch Government. Bets also perceived that one of the Jewish metal merchants by the name of *Cracau* in Terneuzen had asked Kees for refuge on the Scheldestroom. Kees listened carefully to Bets telling him about her Jewish neighbour, an adorable young boy named Victor Walg. His family lived at the Van

Steenberglaan 51; Bets lived at number 57. This boy's family befell grave danger in being deported as she'd noticed one of the Terneuzen NSBers loitering around their house, and it looked ominous. She pleaded with Kees to provide a temporary hiding place on the Scheldestroom. Their secret place was ready; Kees and Francine waited and waited, but sadly they never arrived - too late. To the great dismay of all the neighbours in the van Steenberglaan, the Germans deported the Walg Family to Amsterdam early in March 1942, tragically too early before they could hideaway on the Scheldestroom. On September 3, 1942, they arrived at Dutch transit camp Westerbork, and from there the Nazis took them Auschwitz death camp. Victor and his two brothers, their mum and dad, met their end at Auschwitz on September 7, 1942. As a boy, Tante/*Aunt* Bets told these sweet stories of the little Jewish boy my age. I suspected she would have liked children of her own, but the war put an end to this. She occasionally went walking with Victor and his brothers, and they sailed model sailing boats that Opa Kees had made especially for little boys to sail. Tante Bet's stories made an impact that influenced my spirituality and later norms and values in the way I viewed the world throughout my life.

Werner, an 18-year-old German soldier, was found hiding on the Scheldestroom a few weeks before liberation in September 1944. Francine said, "He suffered terrible flu, and the Krauts would shoot him immediately on suspicion of deserting his post." The family hid him in the fo'c'sle of the Scheldestroom amidst the reserve sails, rope and tar. "That boy has a mother who loves him just like I love my boys," Francine empathised. She imagined Werner to be her boy. "How would I feel if someone saved my boys?"

"Mothers of the world unite," she wrote once. Opa Kees always reminded me that old politicians make war and send mostly innocent and ignorant young men out to fight. When the Germans had retreated, Piet and brother, Kees, delivered Werner to a point in Terneuzen where the Canadians safely transferred him to a prisoner of war camp.

As the occupation continued it became apparent, at least to Kees and Francine, that the Germans were not winning, evidenced by the 24/7 unceasing allied bombing missions to Germany day and night, often flying over the Scheldt at times so densely that the bomber planes blocked out the sunlight over Terneuzen. The Nazis, too, sensed their defeat as did many of the Zealandic Flanders populace. They'd noticed the German's erratic, unpredictable and illogical behaviour and their manifested dejection and dishevelled appearance. Kees said they had lost not only their arrogant confidence but their nerve. Desperate for labour, they began random roundups. They were taking captive unsuspecting young men and boys as young as fourteen from the Terneuzen streets to serve as slaves for the Nazi war machine in Germany. The Paulusses, together with many other good burgers/citizens of Terneuzen, lost no time in hiding their boys, Piet and Kees, with 16 of their friends. Francine recalled," *It was like a Houdini magical vanishing act - all our boys vanished from the streets in less than a nanosecond". She was saying that "the moffen (Krauts) and NSBers were enraged and palpable."* Kees and other skippers silently transported the men in three quiet wooden sailing sloops. There was no fuel for road transport; besides, the Germans and NSBers heavily patrolled the roads. If caught, the boys would be executed immediately on the spot, at least that is what the proclamations issued by the Nazi-sympathising Burgomaster/*mayor* of Terneuzen said. Kees and his brother Bram and several other Skippers took charge of the escape sloops. They knew the waters from Terneuzen to the Emma Polder and the *inundated lands of Safinghe* like the back of their hand. At various points along the River Scheldt, the Dutch underground took the young men taking them to isolated farms deep in the polders. Piet with several others would be hidden in a sheepfold or shearing shed on the inundated lands of Safinghe. Skipper Kees knew his way around these treacherous marshes. As a child, he went there to harvest a variety of sea vegetables. More recently, at the beginning of the war, he led a party that hid valuable machine parts of the ferry boats that plied the Scheldt, so the Germans could not use them. It still surprised him that the Nazis never interrogated him about the whereabouts of his boys. Not surprising because the days were crazy, shown by the events of Tuesday, September 5 1944 – "Dolle Dinsdag"/ *Mad Tuesday*. But he mused that those anxious days were a blessing in disguise. Especially when all the NSBers left in a highly amusing and higgledy-piggledy escape surge, including the Terneuzen Burgomasters and his gang of collaborators.

At the time there was also heavy fighting going on in West Zealandic Flanders where the Germans had 82,000 troops stationed. They had cut the dykes and flooded large parts, hindering the allied advances. Because of heavy fighting on the Scheldt, the war laid up all commercial ships in Terneuzen as the Canadians and Polish forces pushed back the Germans out of Zealandic Flanders. When they got back from hiding their boys, Kees and many other skippers went into hiding themselves. The Germans confiscated their ships to help them escape across the Scheldt to Vlissingen and demanded the skippers to sail them across. They refused and instead went into hiding.

# CHAPTER 8

*He perked up when Francine said intuition told her,*
*'Willemientje ', an endearing pet name for Queen Wilhelmina,*
*will be in Terneuzen tomorrow Tuesday 14 March 1945*

**M**onday 13 March "Kees! Where on earth did you put the six-meter orange pennant the one I made for Princess Juliana's wedding I can't find it". Francine couldn't hide her excitement when a radio bulletin just announced that *Queen Wilhelmina, the symbol of the resistance'* crossed the Dutch border at Eede a village thirty kilometres away from Terneuzen. Adding, and she's visiting the East of Zealandic Flanders too comfort the many victims of devastation and catastrophic war carnage. The many inundated polder villages and towns such as *Breskens* situated at the entrance to the Scheldt estuary bore the brunt of the allied offensive. 'About the orange pennant, Francine called out the second time, "Oh I remember the 'moffen, tore up our tricolour flag during the copper and bronze confiscation razzia, but not the pennant, we're lucky they didn't find it we'd hid it together with the radio". Kees did not respond; he was fixing the hatches damaged badly by large shrapnel; apparently, he often faked deafness when he was focusing on the tasks at hand. He perked up when Francine said intuition told her, 'Willemientje ', an endearing pet name for Queen Wilhelmina, will be in Terneuzen tomorrow Tuesday 14 March.

Just then her youngest brother Hendrik and his wife Marie arrived. The bombardment of Sluiskil had destroyed their Cafe. They were now staying with his elderly mother in the Java Straat. They'd walked down from the Java neighbourhood carrying three bolts of fabric, red white and blue material to make The Netherlands flag. Tante/*Aunt* Leine too is making her way with extra sewing thread she hid during the war, saved for an occasion such as this. Francine recently swapped a bag of potatoes for a new Singer sewing machine, as she did on another occasion you recall, exchanging a bag of food for a Phillips Point radio.

Their excitement and high spirits rose as the flag took its rectangular shape together with other orange buntings, all the while enjoying homemade substitute coffee and spritz cookies that Hendrik had baked. Everybody present hummed *'Het Wilhelmus'* some tried singing it after five years of not singing it. Under occupation, one could land up in a concentration camp for just humming the anthem tune. Still, now they were relieved they could sing to their heart's content, including the oldest national anthem in the world. Later they heard over the radio that the *Terneuzenaren heartedly and with full emotion sang for Wilemientje and feedback indicated that she loved it, Oranjeboven! /Orange Above!* Tears of joy and sadness flowed.

Tuesday 13 March at 7 pm Kees and Francine hoisted the six-meter orange pennant. The homemade red white and blue flag fluttered high in the mast of the Scheldestroom.

Again Francine's intuition was on point; the Queen is coming, the citizens of villages and towns had only 60 minutes to prepare a welcome before her arrival yet the news of her coming travelled fast relayed from house to house, from town crier to town crier. They could not leave the Scheldestroom for security reasons; all the ships enthusiastically flew the flags of the liberation Polish, British, Canadian, French, Belgian American flags everywhere. I still have the tricolour sewed that day on the Scheldestroom. I wonder should I keep it?

Yet there is also much sorrow for the Shipping community when on Dolle Dinsdag/*Mad Tuesday* 5 September 1944 five employees of the

Rijkswaterstaat/*Statewater authority* were executed gruesomely by the Germans for removing dynamite from the locks and bridges around Terneuzen. Everybody in the shipping community knew these brave men personally because they were lock keepers and water engineers who maintained and served the entrance to the Gent Terneuzen sea channel. They were professional, courteous and helpful to the thousands of skippers that passed through their locks every year. Their names never to be forgotten, two water engineers Groenewegen en Hoolsema and three of the lock keepers De Bert, Verbrugge en Nieuwenhuize, Wilhelmina would later meet their widows.

Francine and Kees's favourite nephew, Ko Paulusse a photographer on his way to the town square to welcome Her Majesty diverted his route to join his tante en oom for coffee and spritz in the Scheldestroom Roef. Ko heard they could not leave their ship and agreed to take pictures and afterwards he'd join them for lunch and give a report. Recently, just before Ko's ninety-second birthday, he reminisced to the media about when he stood close to Wilhelmina,

> *"The Queen was visibly touched by the execution of these innocent men. Keeping a distance of three meters and hearing her say in that horrible place of execution near the Western lock: "We must build a memorial on this spot to honour these courageous men"*

And so it happened, the Terneuzen citizens built an impressive monument.

Zealandic Flanders the last to surrender and the first to be liberated. Yet this liberation for the nation ushered in personal turbulence for the Paulusse family a kind of anguish they'd not experienced before. Having already lost their eldest son Jan- Pieter is bad enough, but now all of their sons were at risk serving in the Netherlands Navy and Army. On the day of the Queen's visit, Kees their third son happened to be in Terneuzen on a Dutch navy ship his elder brother Piet is already fighting somewhere in Germany. Many Zealandic Flanders young men voluntary joined the Zealand Battalion in September 1944. Bram their youngest just 17 years old already in the Dutch navy and Kees, both now are on their way to the East Indies.

They were not going alone but with over a thousand other young Dutchmen fighting with the allies defeating the Japanese. Liberating the Dutch East Indies from Japanese oppression and bringing Indonesian collaborators to justice including freeing thousands of Dutch women and children imprisoned in Japanese internment camps or held as hostages by Indonesian Republicans.

Francine's felt the heaviness of heart from the moment her boys left their Scheldestroom home for the last time, more of the agony of mind, the type she had not experienced before. Now all her sons are caught up in the life-threatening theatre of war. It was not the kind of freedom she was expecting she realised not that the nation demanded more of a mother's sacrifice.

Kees more Stoic, trying to keep things to himself was only coping. Yet, his heart too was aching evident by his more than frequent nips of his own distilled Citroen Jenever. Francine referred to it as 'his citroentje for comfort', this type of drink is known to be an excellent tranquilliser, as good as today's Prozac or Valium, it calmed the mind. I remember this Jenever well particularly the considerable length of lemon peel immersed in the transparent yellow Jenever looking more like a work of art, something you want to touch taste and experience. The lemon fragrance was enticingly sweet and warm. After my nagging of giving me a tiny tang they caved in, and as a six-year-old, it was my first and last taste of yellow Jenever. Oh, I'm sure now, they used it as a tranquilliser. On the weekends when friends came to visit they were always greeted by, 'would you like a citroentje first before coffee' that offer was so amiable even teetotalers could not resist.

Kees and fellow Skippers were acting as sea pilots for the Allies on the Scheldestroom as Francine and Leine were providing language translation and Kees helping to mark the locations on maritime maps of treacherous sandbanks on the Scheldt and the Braakman estuaries. Baker Wisse too contributed toward the feeding of all the Soldiers as he said, "who gave us freedom again" and supplied a thousand sausage Rolls made for all the crew on the Scheldestroom. Still, they were not to tell the Canadians or the British that the minced meat was actually horse-meat, as they'd feel disgusted by the idea of eating horse. One of the British officers that came on board for translation services was lieutenant George Penney a long-lost pen pal of Francine's. She had met him at the Hontenisse refugee camp twenty years ago when interned in a Netherlands military internment camp. He had been homesick; the van Aalst sisters had adopted him and a few of the English boys and kept in touch in till the mid-1930's a time to revisit memories. It is always good to have a feast of nostalgia when long-lost friends meet again.

# CHAPTER 9



On a winter's evenings skippers moored next to each other or in the vicinity visited and told their stories.

The ambience in the Roef van de Scheldestroom was the perfect place for hearty conversations and storytelling mixed in the fragrance of sweet toffee pipe tobacco or the pleasing aroma of cigars and Francine's freshly brewed percolated coffee. To get in the mood background music was played from their portable wind up a gramophone record player and an extensive collection of 78rmp records. They did not pay money for it but exchanged it," for a big bag of potatoes somewhere in 'Olland', Francine said, 'because those poor wretches almost died from starvation '.

The family came together whenever they were all in the same port. Francine's youngest sister Marie married Gerrit Tanis, a skipper of an inland oil tanker the Nijverheid. They visited frequently.

Ome Gerrit was a master storyteller always intriguing and found something humourous even in bad situations. The other entertainment factor was in the way he used The Netherlands language. Skippers in the Netherlands spoke in a sort of "skippers" vernacular which could at times be offensive to delicate ears of precious princesses. I remember an adventurous story where he scuttled his inland oil tanker that the Germans were desperate to have. The story he told was titled;

## *The homecoming of Gerrit Tanis*

On "Dolle" Tuesday 14 September 1944 the day the Germans panicked we were moored in Antwerp to anti-magnetize my ship *Nijverheid* against mines. If I had been smart, then I would have deserted the *Nijverheid* and walked from Antwerp all the way to Dendermonde. Instead, Germans came on board and commandeered that I sail the Nijverheid to Wilhelmshaven in Germany. I said to Marie, my wife and daughter Janna" quick pack your essentials" they did not want to leave me, but I insisted. Mother and child left pushing a fully laden pram, looking back with forlorn glances a final hand wave goodbye. Before Marie went, I whispered secretly in her ear to give her the assurance that I was not going to take the Nijverheid to Germany. I would deliberately scuttle her somewhere. In Hansweert harbour I met up with my brother who was skipper of the Luxor the old water supply ship from Terneuzen we met another friend from Oude Tonge and his boat. All three boats together crossed the Eastern Scheld watched by the Germans stationed on our three ships we dared not make any wrong moves. Our lives were at stake. Suddenly Every German ducked for cover because the RAF was doing a lot of shooting, machine-guns, hellish it was. But yes we ended up in the small port at Zijpe, there we spend the whole day hiding in ditches because English planes kept coming over the Grevelingen. They machine-gunned the Germans continually, anything that floated.

In the evening, we had to get out of our safe ditches. That was not easy because the Germans jumped on every ship, including our vessels and even more reinforcements came inboard when we reached Oude Tonge. Fighting intensified the whole Sky was lit up like daylight even more so when the English use light flares to give them a clear view of what was happening on the ground. We jumped ashore hiding together while cannon fire remained unceasingly. We hatched our plan of escape knowing full well that if caught we'd be executed on the spot. The Germans were shitting themselves jumping ship and just left us there. They briefly returned after a few hours, but I told them it wasn't safe to continue as the English had parachuted magnetic mines. We'd all lose our lives blown to smithereens if we hit a mine. I thought then we would scuttle all three ships here at the *Moerdijk*. All German gunfire had stopped they had made a run for it, and we too made a getaway. We sheltered in a German fox hole complete with machine guns and bullets ready to shoot. Of course, we were not going to stay there and moved on, under cover of darkness.

Arriving at the small village *Dinteloord* just at daybreak, there was not a mortal to be seen, we waited for nothing, but nothing happened. My brother and I packed some food and clothes, we told the other men that we were going for groceries, milk and such, that was good. I told them we'll be back when it is dark. We left. Then we walked deep into the polder at a deserted farm which was half underwater. It was in the Herkingse polder, near Stampersgat.

The water level was already high, the moffen had dynamite some dykes flooding the holders. We stayed there for about three days, we had to get out because we had nothing to eat. At night we crawled into the apple trees in the orchard looking for apples. We had found a jar of pickles, but there were six of us, so we are pickles and apples only. You shouldn't overthink about that. We stayed in that wet Barn attic for fourteen days. Sleeping on straw taken out of the feeding trays of cow but the lice, millions of lice that are us alive! To get rid of them we wet our hair and comb your hair, the trouble was we only had one

I met comb and one toothbrush for the six of us; frankly, it was more like a zoo on our heads.

One morning sitting around listening to the wind it had been stormy weather. Oh yes, I have to tell you, we carried a book of cards with us. We are sitting there playing cards on that island when suddenly we hear the outside door squeaking. Hey, what is that? My brother jumps up and silently heads to the attic stairs, and he sees a man walking away, closing the door behind him. But he quickly returns, my brother opens the door, and there is a farmer outside. That man asks, "what are you guys doing here? We said we had gone into hiding. He says I came here to close the door of this shed because it has blown open. We knew that but yes we did not come down when it was not necessary and also not outside, because of the water and we don't want to drown. He says I cannot do anything for you. I have had Jews hiding here, but I don't want any more anxiety caused by hiding people and endangering the safety of my family. We knew the story about the Jews was real because that attic was made in such a way that a sizeable secret room is hidden behind bookshelves filled with books. There we found those pickles and also a paraffin cooking set. We had converted the hideout so that we could quickly flee in it when the Germans came doing razzia.

That farmer said he could not do anything, so there we anxiously awaiting we sat when around nine o'clock in the evening there was another knock. We thought that the dirty farmer had betrayed us. Nothing of the sort it was his brother with a massive 12-litre milk jug, three wheat loaves and a pound of butter. We were so thankful and felt we were getting somewhere. One of us came from *Oudetonge* and was well known in that polder. One morning he says, "I will explore the polder" There he came into contact with a certain Bousche van *Breskens* in Zealandic Flanders. He has secreted away ton a houseboat. His ship had sunk on the Braakman. Me Bousche offered to prepare is a large cauldron of potatoes carrots and onions. He fulfilled his promise and brought the warm food to us in the evening, raising our spirits on Sunday morning. Hundreds of glider planes flew over—an incredible sight. One of the gliders was shot down and crashed in the back paddock we couldn't go there because we'd drown besides we expect the Moffen/*Krauts* at any moment, but they did not come. That plane, we knew it was there, but you didn't see anything it was half underwater partly floating. In the morning I went there at 4 am with that friend from *Oude Tonge*. I thought, "if they come, then we will be there, so well escape. Apparently, the pilots were already rescued by the underground.

We had to leave this place as the Germans would eventually come looking for the crashed glider.

We hit the road again. We knocked on the door of another farmhouse in another polder. The farmer and his wife were eating. There was so much vermin in his house there that you couldn't see his eyes from the flies. Never seen a household like this, but we were invited to share their food, when you're hungry, you cannot be fussy.

T "was a real Brabanter. We got a little fold for on the way, as we were about to leave he introduces us to a certain Mr Scheele, who to our delight came from Axel a town near Terneuzen. He was in the underground. We made an appointment to see him. When we got to his

the place he wasn't there, his wife prepared food for us. We told them our story and who we were. She said she would try to do something for us. Well and so we had to find our way back to our birds' nest in the polder again. The four guys we're expecting us back in the evening. So we arrived also as promised. At the village of Standaard, we met a farmer with a couple of horses and cart. Hey, he says to hop on the cart, and he'll bring us to the Standaard Town Hall where we are going to commit a burglary he laughs. We enter the building meeting officials, asking us how many bread ration cards do you need how many coupons? They offered to bring us back to our place of shelter on the back of the cart, but that would have been too risky as people could see us, strangers. No, it was not possible to travel with horse and cart most of the Polders were partially inundated beside it would be risky. Everyone would see us and know where our hiding place was. I said we will work it out ourselves, as long as we know where we have to go. So we returned to our men. We explained the whole situation to the underground people. The next morning at about six o'clock two people arrived in waders, one of them was called Mr Dis, they came to say that we had to go there and there in the evening. We walked everywhere diving in ditches, not wanting to be seen that night we hid in a school. The German soldiers had quartered there before us leaving everything behind beds and blankets, pots and pans. We took the useful stuff to our new hiding place a windmill alongside a potato warehouse with a heater. We made a whole room out of these boxes, including cribs to sleep it was comfortable and stayed for two months at a place called Fijnaard. The Miller/ farmer was delighted to have six men working for him we slaughtered, we harvested dug out acres of sugar beet and picked potatoes. That farmer said we could do anything, Yes probably he was happy, my brother plastered and painted his kitchen. That farmer had thirty fish traps, and I was in charge of catching fish. We stayed there until the liberation. Then I went home to Terneuzen.

Getting back home to Terneuzen was a big problem as public transport and ferry services were severely damaged. The moffen had blown up all the bridges and overpasses. But arriving at Baarland, I couldn't go any further because Jan Jongman and Klaasje Quellerri no longer operated the ferries. Still, they secretly used their privately own fishing boats. Besides the allies had forbidden to cross the Scheld on account of the many mines. Damn what now? There were a lot of people waiting to catch the ferry at Baarland. Still, no one could get over to Zealandic Flanders. I wanted to see Mr Sandpot, the commander of the Scheldt guard, occupying the house of the harbour master. Also waiting to see him was a woman with a child from Tholen whose husband worked on one of the minesweepers. He had spent a good many years in England and is now clearing mines in Terneuzen harbour. She wanted to go to her man, but she could not get over either, she too approached the harbour master who asked me if I was willing to take the risk in using the large

Pilot rowing sloop." You're a skipper, right? he said," will you take the risk and care are you daring enough to row the pilot's sloop to Terneuzen. I said yes I'm bold, but one thing there can't be too many people in the boat, because when that boat is overloaded in rough seas, everyone will drown.

And you know when that boat is ready, everybody will try and jump in. I don't like it because people have just as much right as I do. I will take care of that, says the commander. Anyway, it all went well, but we were not even five hundred meters outside the harbour when one those minesweepers from Terneuzen came alongside our sloop. Yes, where do you have to go with his rowboat full of people...the ebb current pulled is away in the right direction with speed four men were rowing, but the waves were high.

The woman from *Tholen* was on board with her really seasick child we rolled the eight-year-old boy up in blankets. The sloop was taking in a lot of water, I said to the men we can make it as long as you guys scoop the water out and then we'll get on the other side. With the tide quickly pushing us to our destination we finally arrived at De Eendracht east of Terneuzen. It's quite an achievement to cross the Western Scheld in stormy weather crossing tricky sandbanks floating mines.

The People became excited as soon as they saw the dykes and said, skipper, we have gone far enough let us disembarked on the dike. I say no we have to continue to the harbour at Griete were it is safe to land, if you land here on the dike, we will bet smashed to smithereens, and we'll all drown. We kept rowing briefly below the dike and arrived at the Griete. Then we still had to go home. Those of the PZEM took the sick boy with them on their bicycles to Terneuzen. I walked to Terneuzen across the Axel bridge and into the street near us, Just at dusk. Our Janna was standing outside she calls There's pappa. I was home again.

*About Ome/uncle Gerrit.*

Gerrit Tannis was just 7 years old when his mother died. His father, a fisherman by trade, was left with 6 children. These children were housed with relatives. Gerrit was raised by his uncle Dirk's Aunt Jacomijntje (Mientje) Tanis at 53 Hazersweg.

Gerrit started sailing on inland shipping at a young age for a Belgian shipping company.

He made it to Captain of an inland tanker the "Nijverheid" with a three-cylinder Kromhout of 120hp. Loading took place in Antwerp or Rotterdam and unloaded in Zeebrugge or Ostend.

After the marriage of Gerrit, Marie came to live on board. Two of the three children worked as a deckhand with Gerrit. The family thus formed the crew of the ship, and it was not necessary to employ strangers.

During the war, Gerrit was required like everybody else to sail for the Germans. At the end of 1944, Gerrit de "Nijverheid" and his brother Willem, who also had a ship, we're forced by the Germans to Germany. In Brabant, they left their boats and went into hiding with a farmer in Fijnaart. They stayed with this farmer until the liberation.

# EPILOGUE SCHELDESTROOM

The end of the war brought neither relief, nor peace of mind for Francine and Kees their days of turmoil increased. There were labour shortages, Kees's elder brother 76-year-old Bram whose ship the Nazis confiscated "Elizabeth" returned to work as a deckhand on the Scheldestroom.

As soon as the Allies liberated Zealandic Flanders in September 1944, their remaining three boys volunteered for the Netherlands Navy and Army in supporting the Allies with their push into Germany. After the German surrender, the three sons were sent to the Dutch East Indies to help defeat the Japanese. They were stoic despite their constant worry; in the back of their mind, they had not forgotten the Battle of the Java Sea we're over 2.300 Dutch and allied sailors lost their young lives.

The Paulusse family, like many other families, had a stake in the future of The Netherlands. They kept abreast of political and economic developments through reading and discussions. They were never a superficial couple fortifying their minds through critically thinking; consequently, the vicissitudes of life did not daunt them. Francine purchased every book that was published about the work and progress the Zealand Battalion (2-14R.I.) was making in the Dutch East Indies. These books abounded with many photos of new hospitals, food distribution centres, transportation ships carrying rōmushas and the liberated Dutch and allied prisoners of war back to Indonesia.

The idea that their sons were doing humanitarian instead of waging war appealed and instilled some psychological comfort. It was true that their boys were not in Indonesia to preserve colonial status. Dutch troops in Indonesia were busy bringing back to Indonesia the millions of rōmushas the forced labourers provided to the Japanese by the collaborators such as Sukarno. The rule of law had to be applied. British and Dutch troops liberated the Japanese Internment camps containing thousands of Dutch women and their children. After the Japanese surrendered, these internees were held to ransom by the Indonesian Republicans. The Indonesian populace had little food, and the Dutch brought in food, medical supplies and rebuilt hospitals. Their surmising of humanitarian work is supported by UN statistic. *The report stated that 4 million people died in Indonesia as a result of the Japanese occupation. About 2.4 million people died in Java from famine during 1944- 45.*

The plan was that they would soon retire and Piet would purchase the Scheldestroom when he came back from the war. Piet arrived back from Indonesia in 1948 while his brothers Kees and Bram remained in that theatre of war until 1950. None of the boys wanted to sail the Scheldestroom she was too much work, besides the girlfriends of Kees and Piet didn't want to be shippers wives. The decision was made in 1949 to sell the Scheldestroom. The new owners maintained the name Scheldestroom and lengthened her by about 5 meters and converted to a motor ship. They officially retired purchasing two houses in Dahlia street Terneuzen renting out one place for a retirement income. Because they were not eligible for any state-funded pensions, that would come later.

On 16 July 1957 Bram, their twenty-eight-year-old son died in a KLM Super Constellation (Royal Dutch Airlines) Flight 844 crashing into Cenderawasih Bay 1.3 kilometres (0.75 mi) from Biak departure airport in former Dutch New Guinea. Resulting in the loss of, 58 (9 of which were crew members) out of 68 people on board perished.

They were further pained when Piet and his family migrated to Australia in 1961. I wrote Vertek a book about our migration to Australia. Kees married Dolly and moved to Haarlem their two daughters Janna and Bette with their families stayed in Terneuzen.

The past continues to speak and encourage us today. I value the long-ago letters and postcards sent to me by my four omas and opas, family and friends. Even after decades, I still touch and smell some of the perfume or cigar fragrance of loved ones permeated into their notes. When feeling forlorn, I re-read the positive written affirmations on these cards. Especially those of my many aunties and Grandparents they always started with "lieve Kees" "Darling Keith" powerful affirmations that saw me through times of personal hardships and trauma. Glad I kept those written memories in a shoebox instead of them digitally floating around the ether merged and lost with trillions of other messages. Sadly nowadays there are few shoe boxes laden with postcards and letters.

For 40 years the Paulusse family had floated on water living on the Scheldestroom sailing on rivers and seas often against the wind. Theirs was not a stay-put neighbourhood, yet they knew every skipper family as though they were next-door neighbours. Theirs was one of perpetual change; there was rarely the same location or scenery; every day, a storm could happen. Change like the weather was their only constant in life, adjustment their saviour. Now they retired to permanent onshore living a significant event of transition and assimilation. Suddenly there was one house one neighbourhood seeing the same neighbours day in and day out was a novelty. Yet they did not miss meeting exciting people in their new onshore home. Their warm hospitality attracted an endless variety of engaging visitors, especially the international buyers for Kees's vintage ships. Presently they maintained their window on world events on science the arts and literature through the medium of TV being one of the first in the Netherlands to purchase a TV back in 1952.

Francine passed on in 1962 from gall bladder complications still too young at 74 years. I visited Opa Kees in 1968 he was happily living with Jana his second daughter who far too early, passed away, age 48.

It was then that Kees moved to an Aged Care Facility. His letters to me indicated that he liked socialising. It is all a matter of adjusting to change the only constant in our lives. Cornelis Paulusse passed away aged 86 in 1972.

They left their footprints on the earth; their spiritual presence can still be felt. Francine and Kees were not superficial types. Consequently, they were seldom put off by the vicissitudes of life; they realized that knowledge is the power to live useful lives in abundance, and they did. My ancestors are not forgotten. One is only dead when you are lost in the collective memory.

# Nederlandse Scheldestroom

## Sammenvatting van Hoofstuk inhoud.

INVOERING

* Historisch. De Bronnen van de Scheldestroom
* Onderzoekers groep

HOOFDSTUK 1

* De Zusjes van Aalst naar Londen
* Nederlandse directheid in communicatie met de Engelsen
* Ontmoeting Emmeline n Panhurst en schrijfster Virginia Wolf
* Ze gingen veel naar de shows in het West end.
* Ontmoeting met meneer Boot, scheepsbouwer van snelle gracieuze Klippers
* Londense warenhuizen waren een "paradijs voor dames'

HOOFDSTUK 2

* De drie gebroerders Paullusse op bezoek in 1900 aan het "Paris Exposition Universelle"
* Terug van Parijs de broeders waren omgetovert tot visionairen,innovators, ondernemers en vooral kritische denkers
* De reis van Terneuzen naar Delft nam vier uur.Ze hadden een borgsom van 1500 gulden.De Scheldestroom gebout en gedoopt.
* Groot vervoer contract voor stenen.
* De zeilen van de Scheldestroom waren van hennep.Een bezoek aan de hennep velden van Nederland.

HOOFDSTUK 3

* De Grote Oorlog begint, Nederland neutraal
* Er werd een gemeenschapsoproep gedaan naar de inwoners van Terneuzen om de duizenden Belgische vluchtelingen te helpen

- Scheldestroom redt Belgische vlugtelingen.
- De zusjes van Aalst doen vrijwilligerswer in het vluchtelingenkamp Hontenisse
- Ze waren dankbaar voor hun grote en gezellige Roef waar 9 mensen comfortabel konden wonen
- Er weinig of geen hulp was van de Nederlandse regering voor de eerste megagolven van vluchtelingen.

## HOOFDSTUK 4

- Het vervoer van buitenlandse geïnterneerde militairen
- Engelse jongens leken zo verloren en verbijsterd en leeg, ze konden niet geloven dat het machtige Engeland op dat moment verslagen was.
- Hij was altijd bang was dat de Engelsen, Duitsers of de Amerikanen zijn schip op volle zee zouden stelen
- Francine nam het stuur over en Kees stelde de zeilen om de volle wind snelheid te krijgen. De race begon
- Kees kon zich niet herinneren hoeveel vliegtuigen hij van Cadzand met de Scheldestroom had vervoerd.

## HOOFDSTUK 5

- De roaring twenties Scheldestroom welvaart en nieuwe technologie
- De geboorte vab drie zonen
- Stenen and Zeeuws voedsel voor de IX Olympische Spelen in Amsterdam

## HOOFDSTUK 6

- Scheldestroom in de cricis jaren. De depressie van 1930
- Vernietigin door de Nederlandse Regeering van tonnen groente.
- Aardappelen naar aangewezen geheime pakhuizen smokkelen voor de hongerige bevolking.

# INVOERING

## De historische bronnen voor de Scheldestroom

Toen mijn ouders Piet en Bets hun 60ste huwelijksverjaardag bereikten, besloot ik om elk weekend samen met hen door te brengen in hun huis bovenop de Leopoldheuvel in Victoria.

Als het mooi weer was, gingen we vaak voor korte autoritten, picknicks of een bezoek aan enkele van hun oudere vrienden. We praatten over alles van vroeger en over hun toekomstige bestemming. Ze waren altijd geïnteresseerd in het leven, en waren niet bang voor de toekomst omdat ze uit het verleden hadden geleerd dat angst voor het denkbeeldige onbekende een zware psychologische last is.

Bij moeder Bets werd vijf jaar eerder de ziekte van Alzheimer vastgesteld. Ze had weinig of geen kortetermijngeheugen meer, haar langetermijngeheugen was intact. Piet had milde Parkinson, maar met medicatie werden de slopende effecten getemperd. Al snel moest ik mijn baan opzeggen en bij hen intrekken, omdat hun toestand langzaam achteruitging. Bijna drie jaar was ik op pas bij hen totdat ze stierven. Piet en ik spraken veel over zijn vormingsjaren op het schip van zijn geboorte de Scheldestroom, de economische depressie van de jaren dertig, de invasie en vijandelijke bezetting van Nederland, zijn militaire dienst in Bataljon Zeeland 2/14 RI, de Politie-actie in de Interventie in Indonesië, zijn liefde voor Bets, de geboorte van zijn kinderen en natuurlijk de migratie naar Australië.

Bets volgde onze gesprekken via de vele fotoalbums van de verschillende periodes van de Paulusse clan en ons collectieve gezinsleven. Haar langetermijngeheugen was scherp, dus ze herinnerde zich gebeurtenissen snel zodra ze een foto in de fotoalbums zag en nam gretig deel aan de gesprekken en herinnerde zich gebeurtenissen. Behalve de fotoalbums waren er een duizendtal ansichtkaarten en brieven, allemaal gestapeld in verschillende schoenendozen, van meer dan honderd jaar terug. We hadden ze herlezen en meer dan vaak de goede en minder mooie momenten opnieuw beleefd. Ansichtkaarten zijn als een tijdscapsule van tijd en ruimte met details over gebeurtenissen van de Scheldestroom en de mensen die op haar leefden.

We hebben een duizendtal boeken in onze familie bibliotheek die van generatie op generatie werd overgedragen. Onlangs heb ik nog meer materiaal gevonden dat licht werpt op de Scheldestroom. Mijn grootouders en mijn vader, ontdekte ik verrukkelijk, hadden de gewoonte om verrassende dingen tussen de boekpagina's te stoppen. Artikelen zoals persoonlijke brieven, krantenknipsels en handgetekende ontwerpschetsen van de Scheldestroom droegen bij aan mijn intriges en motivatie. Deze vondsten hadden allemaal betrekking op de verschillende perioden van het leven van de Scheldestroom. Ik realiseerde me toen dat het verhaal van de Scheldestroom een historische thriller is die de hele twintigste eeuw omvat.

Een verdere impuls voor het schrijven van het verhaal over de Scheldestroom begon toen mijn neef Andre de Groot mijn aandacht vestigde op een voormalig klipper zeilschip dat te koop was in Nederland. Zie, daar was de 110 jaar oude Scheldestroom gedetailleerd met veel foto's. Weliswaar gemoderniseerd, verlengd en gemotoriseerd maar toch herkenbaar aan haar knappe boeg en achtersteven. Ze werd verkocht en het plan van de nieuwe eigenaren is om het schip in zijn oude zeilglorie te herstellen.

Elk commercieel schip in Nederland is verplicht om een vrachtmanifest te hebben. Omdat Opa Kees een Nederlander is, hield hij deze en de winst- en verlies- en uitgavenadministratie nauwgezet bij. Zelf heb ik al deze originelen in mijn bezit. Toen ik de inhoud van al deze documenten met mijn vader besprak, had hij voor elk item een verhaal. Ik schreef al zijn herinneringen op, niet op een droge, saaie manier, maar met woorden die de emotie van die tijd uitdrukten.

Bij het schrijven van Scheldestroom heb ik moderne sociologische, psychologische en medische termen gebruikt die in 1910 nog niet bestonden. Bijvoorbeeld; 'De zussen van Aalst beschikten over een hoge mate van *emotionele intelligentie*'. En voor mijn grootouders hadden een waardevol *'sociaal kapitaal'*, dat wil zeggen netwerken van relaties tussen mensen met wie ze in hun samenleving leefden, waardoor die samenleving effectief kon functioneren. Verschillende van mijn relaties in het verhaal van de Scheldestroom leden aan psychische problemen, die ik op de juiste manier interpreteerde op basis van mijn psychologische studies als *bipolair* of zo en zo op het *autismespectrum*.

Het idee van de Scheldestroom begon toen de drie Paulusse bros, opgewonden en hergebruikt terugkeerden van de 'Paris Exposition Universelle' van 1900. Gelijktijdig met de terugkeer van de zusjes van Aalst van hun twee jaar werkervaring in Londen. De restanten van hun ervaringen en wat ze hebben geleerd, maakten hen tot visionaire vernieuwers, ondernemers en kritische denkers die hun toekomst voor de komende 100 jaar bedachten. Scheldestroom is de belichaming van de twintigste eeuw. Te water gelaten in 1910 en zeilend over 100 jaar door al de uitdagingen en kansen en overgangen tijdens de conflicten van de twintigste eeuw. Scheldestroom is een werk van non-fictie waarvan het verhaal in feite is gebaseerd. We komen het dichtst bij de werkelijke tijdreizen. Het is een historische thriller van de twintigste eeuw, niet verteld of geschreven door academici, maar door gewone mensen. Gebaseerd op honderden briefkaarten, kranten knippsels vrachtmanifesten en mondelinge interviews en anekdotes.

Mijn verhaal van de Scheldestroom is avontuurlijk en motiverend, het leest als een roman die altijd wordt verteld door *mijn stroom van bewustzijn*, dat is mijn manier om verhalen te vertellen, maar het is geen versie van een academisch boek dat voor altijd verwijst naar deze bron endat bron. Nee! mijn verhaal is echt, zelfs ideaal, want er is niets slechts of valse kunstmatig gegenereerd sensationeel drama. Maar er is opwinding en veel intriges zoals Kees die verliefd wordt op Francine, zonder deze liefde had de Scheldestroom niet bestaan. Ik zou zeker niet hebben bestaan. De Britse marine die de Scheldestroom achtervolgde tijdens de Eerste Wereldoorlog, het transport van duizend Belgische vluchtelingen, of het vervoeren van een Britse marinebrigade naar Nederlandse interneringskampen. Of de bijna-confiscatie door de Gestapo van de inbeslagname van de Scheldestroom of de geheime bouw voor een onderduikadres voor Joodse vrienden, of de verandering van taak en opbouw van de Scheldestroom tijdens de Grote Depressie. Een nog betere vraag is hoe een gezin van tien, acht kinderen en twee ouders tot bloei kwam in een zeer kleine woonruimte in de Roef.

Hoe overleefden ze door tyfus en de Spaanse griep? Hoe hebben ze de moeilijke tijden doorstaan zonder kinderbijslag of overheidsuitgaven, hoe hebben ze honderden tonnen vracht door West-Europa vervoerd zonder motor, alleen zeilen en wind, het klinkt allemaal onwerkelijk, daarom moest het verhaal van de Scheldestroom worden verteld, hier is het en het leeft.

Pasen 1968 was de laatste keer dat ik mijn 84 jaar Opa Cornelis Paulusse zag. Iedereen noemde hem Kees. Ik ben naar hem vernoemd, net als andere kleinzonen. Voordat ik terugkeerde naar Australië, bracht ik met hem enkele dagen door met fietsen door de oude polders van Zeeuws-Vlaanderen over de dijken met gigantische wilgen en populieren. Hij nam me mee naar historische dorpen met hun oude ingezande door de tijd verloederde haventjes. Samen fietsen we naar plaatsen die belangrijk waren voor de natievorming, niet alleen voor Nederland, maar ook voor de wereld waaraan de familie Paulusse net als anderen had bijgedragen. Ik zeg anderen, tenminste als ze historische voetstappen hebben achtergelaten.

## Scheldestroom in de Nederlandse taal

Ik kwam als elfjarige jongen naar Australië, de spreektaal van mijn familie was Zeeuws-Vlaams. Nadat ik in november 1961 in Australië aankwam, kwam er abrupt een einde aan mijn formele Nederlandse taalopleiding. Mijn boek- en krantenlezen ging echter door in de Nederlandse taal en thuis spraken we altijd de Zeeuws-Vlaamse taal die alleen veranderde als andere Nederlanders kwamen sprakten we de officiële Nederlandse taal of te wel *Algemeen Beschaaft Nederlands* noemden ze dat, maar met de veele vloeken en tieren die daar door ingemengd werden vond ik er niet veel beschaafts aan. *Dus de Zeeuwse taele is de mooiste taele van oalemale vonden wij.*

Ik bied absoluut geen excuses aan voor mijn naoorlogse Nederlandse immigrantentaal uit de jaren '60 met de bijbehorende Spreuken - Idioom - Gezegden - Woordspelingen - Aforismen, noch voor de lokale Zeeuws-Vlaamse unieke uitdrukking en proza-, evenals syntaxis die mogelijk niet overeenkomt met de aanvaarde Nederlands taalnormen. But who cares? als het maar gezellig gemoedelijk en vrolijk is zeg ik altijd.

Ik vind het troost om te weten dat ik in goed gezelschap ben van mede-Zeeuwse Vlaamse taalkundigen, zoals *Johan Hendrik van Dale*, een eenmalige schoolleraar in de binnenstad van Sluis, wiens driedelige Lexicografie het grootste Woordenboek van de Nederlandse taal is, in het algemeen bekend als de 'Dikke van Dale', het 'Humungousvan Dale'. Dan is er *Marnix van St Aldegonde* die net als ik Zeeuws-Vlaams sprak en het oudste en voortdurende volkslied ter wereld schreef: "Het Wilhelmus". Een andere Zeelander die in de volkstaal sprak, was

*Jacob Cats* een bekende Nederlandse dichter, humorist, jurist en politicus, hij is in heel Nederland bekend als Vader Cats, Dichter van de natie. Een meer eigentijdse Zealander was *Annie GM Schmidt*, een Zeeuwse kinderschrijver, toneelschrijver van talloze musicals die ze nu is opgenomen in het 'Kanon van de Nederlandse geschiedenis, naast nationale iconen als Vincent van Gogh en Anne Frank. Dus ik ben in goed gezelschap.

## Bedankt aan het Scheldestroom Research Team

Louis van der Hooft.

Visuele verteller, mondelinge historicus. Ik zou niet zijn begonnen met het schrijven van Scheldestroom zonder Loius 'historisch archief met duizenden oude foto's, ansichtkaarten, brieven, artefacten, filmpjes van de Zeeuwse havenstad Terneuzen. Zijn verzameling van grote en kleine gebeurtenissen over het dagelijks leven. Vastgelegd met behulp van geluidsbanden, videoclips en transcripties van interviews hielpen mij enorm. Vaak heb ik de Scheldestroom opgemerkt in zijn archief of een ver familielid zien deelnemen aan een werkelijke historische gebeurtenis waarin mijn voorouders betrokken waren. Door het opwindende archief van Louis te bekijken, voelde ik me verbonden met het verleden en gaven mij de sleutels tot de toekomst.

Andre de Groot

Andre is mijn achterneef en schipper van een 450 ton wegende schip de "Unicum". Hij heeft historische documenten, foto's en krantenartikelen over Scheldestroom achterna gezeten. Ook bezocht en fotografeerde hij de Scheldestroom op de scheepswerf van Harlingen, waar Scheldestroom hopelijk in haar oorspronkelijke vaarvermogen word hersteld.

Patricia Paulusse

Mijn night een beeldend kunstenaar, en mijn go-to adviseur van alles wat met Nederland te maken heeft. Zij heeft geduldig he Scheldestroom manuscript gelezen en beleefde aanbeveling voor verbetering, zonder mijn stem te verliezen.

Walter en Elly Hes

Deze Australiësche na oorlogse Nederlandse migrantenpaar zowel schrijvers als auteurs. Hielpen mij met het luisteren naar ideeën en concepten. Ze fungeerden als een juichend aanmoedigingsteam. Ze hielden van het soort Nederlands dat ik spreek dit gaf mij vertrouwen in het schrijven van dit tweetalig boek

Kai Jiang; my former student and now friend a Portrait Artist voor het protet van Francine, en andere Scheldestroom mommenten..

Met dank aan *Poolster Charters* in Harlingen Nederland voor de foto van de zeilende Poolster River klipper image.

# HOOFSTUK 1

*De van Aalst Zusters het jaar 1906*
*Deze urbane jonge van Aalst-vrouwen uit Zeeuws-Vlaanderen*
*trokken de aandacht van zeekapiteins en diplomaten*

Francine en Leine werden naar Engeland uitgezwaaid door hun vader Jan van Aalst en hun vriend Cornelis Paulusse, gewoonlijk Kees genaamd, die hen naar Vlissingen zeilden op het schip van zijn vader een 140 ton zware houten cargo Tjalk *"De Vertrouwen"*, die schuin van Terneuzen de woelige en winderige wateren van de beroemde Westerschelde overstak naar Vlissingen, een zeiltocht van 90 minuten tegen de wind. In Vlissingen gingen de twee van Aalst dames aan boord van de *Prins Hendrik*, een stoom radar schip, dat over een uur of negen in Londen veilig zou aankomen. Tenminste, dat hoopten ze want het weer was slecht.

Woensdag 11 april 1906 was een ijskoude ochtend toen de mooie 17-jarige Francine samen met haar aantrekkelijke oudere zus Leine aan boord van de Prins Hendrik stapte één van de luxe raderstoombooten die hen in minder dan negen uur naar Londen zou brengen over de Noordzee.

Veel van de Zeeuws-Vlaamse jonge vrouwen gingen buiten hun huis werken en gingen zelfs naar het buitenland voor avontuur, zoals moderne back packers van vandaag dat ook doen en vinden banen zoals au pairs, dienstmeisjes, gastvrouwen, barmeisjes of zelfs bordeelmeisjes.

Ze kregen zelfs een gelijk inkomen en waren niet zozeer afhankelijk van het inkomen van hun familie of echtgenoten. Dit was in Zeeuws-Vlaanderen de regel, niet zo veel elders in Nederland waar de religieuze cohorten mannen stevig boven vrouwen werden geplaatst, maar meestal niet in verlichte seculiere kringen.

Francine en Leine hadden een baan aangeboden gekregen omdat ze meertalig waren en een hoge mate van *emotionele intelligentie* hadden, om nog maar te zwijgen van hun uiterlijk. Beiden hadden een goed gevoel voor humor en zorgden er voor dat iedereen zich op zijn gemak en betrokken voelde.

Hun formele opleiding eindigde op 14-jarige leeftijd en ze begonnen op die jonge leeftijd te werken, als dienstmeisjes in de Zeeuwse Haven stad Terneuzen. Er waren zes meisjes in de familie van Aalst; Francine, Sophia, Leine, Marie, Lena en Jane. En twee broers, Piet en de knappe Hendrik de jongste. In totaal acht broers en zussen, 11 als we de drie stil geboren baby's meetellen. Ze hadden allemaal beschrijvende bijnamen van vertedering. Vader, Jan van Aalst was een laagbetaalde arbeider en soms matroos, werkend in een houtfabriek. Hij trouwde met Jana Harte, een hoedenmaakster. Ze woonden in de nette arbeidersbuurt genaamd "Java" op Java Straat 32 in Terneuzen.

Het maakte niet uit dat de familie van Aalst economisch arm was, veel belangrijker was dat ze fysiek en mentaal gezond waren, dat blijkt uit het feit dat de meeste broers en zussen tot hoge leeftijd leefden. Jan en Janna van Aalst vierden hun vijftigste huwelijksverjaardag in 1936 in hun Java-familiehuis tussen hun vele kleinkinderen die voor het grootste deel in het verhaal van De Scheldestroom voorkomen. Ik heb een foto geplaatst van hun jubileum wat onder familie gevierd werd.

Ik herinner me dat ik als kind luisterde naar oma Francine die leesboeken besprak met haar broers en zussen, die allemaal de hele tijd lid waren geweest van muziek, toneel en beeldende kunstverenigingen, waardoor ze niet leden aan onwetendheid of vooroordelen over matheid of gebrek aan creativiteit en er bleek altijd energie te zijn voor "sta op en ga."

Veel van de Zeeuws-Vlaamse families waren behoorlijk geavanceerd en bezaten veel *sociaal kapitaal* verworven in de pluralistische multiculturele havengemeenschap, zoals Terneuzen, het centrale punt van internationale activiteit die Antwerpen, Gent en Brugge met elkaar verbindt in een radius van ongeveer 35 kilometer. Niet alleen wereldberoemde havensteden zijn het maar ook eeuwenlang de culturele centra van Europa, zelfs aan het begin van de 19e eeuw. Het was heel anders in de rest van Nederland, waar mensen meestal in hun sektarische bubbels woonden en zich zelden uit hun dorp of steden waagden. Antwerpen beroemd gemaakt door *Peter Paul Rubens* en Brugge en Gent door *Jan van Eyck* en niet te vergeten de diamanthoofdstad van de wereld daarvoor een multiculturele gemeenschap van ouds af aan.

Het leven in zo'n multiculturele en pluralistische samenleving gaf veel Zeeuws-Vlaamse vrouwen een gezond zelfvertrouwen en eigenwaarde, waardoor ze hun *intra-persoonlijk* begrip ontwikkelden, in tegenstelling tot de vermeende onderdrukking van vrouwen elders in Europa en of in Nederland.

Deze urbane jonge van Aalst-vrouwen en andere vrouwen uit Zeeuws-Vlaanderen trokken de aandacht van zeekapiteins en diplomaten die in deze havensteden gestationeerd waren, waaronder een Charles Van Gyzelen die enige tijd chef-kok was bij Hotel Rotterdam in Terneuzen. Het was Charles die Francine en Leine bemoedigden om daar te gaan solliciteren als gastvrouwen voor internationale gasten in het luxueuze *Ritz Hotel* dat op 6 juni 1906 zou openen.

De meisjes spraken perfect Frans, Engels en Duits, evenals Nederlands ... in eerste instantie waren ze al geaccepteerd om aan het werk te gaan als dienstmeisjes voor zeer rijke Engelse mensen, waaronder de familie van de gewaardeerde *Lord Kitchener*. Het gerucht ging dat Kitchener niet bepaald gesteld was op Nederlandse vrouwen of welke vrouw dan ook, en de voorkeur gaf aan het gezelschap van jonge mannen als bedienden. Bovendien was de Boerenoorlog net vijf jaar eerder afgelopen en waren de Engelsen nog steeds hun wonden aan het likken van hun recente 65.000 slachtoffers en de 55.000 Britse soldaten gesneuveld door een Boerenleger dat zich *'guerrillastrijders'* noemden.

"De Boeren zijn onze eigenzinnige neven en nichten "zei Francine en vertelde mij het met een knipoog; ze kreeg lucht van Kitcheners afkeer van de Boeren en hun verre familie de Nederlanders. Dus ze weigerden de banen van Kitchener en accepteerden de functies bij *Ritz Hotel*. Er zijn in die tijd veel verhalen over het Ritz, maar dat is niet de bedoeling van dit boek.

Het andere aspect van het werken, naast het opdoen van waardevolle levenservaring in Londen, was het verdienen van graag veel geld. Het leven draait vooral om het belang van geld krijgen. Ze zouden goed geld verdienen. Zowel Kees Paulusse als Francine van Aalst hadden in het geheim al over het huwelijk gesproken zonder dat iemand op de hoogte was van hun bedoeling. Voordat ze gingen trouwen, besloten ze te sparen voor een fatsoenlijke aanbetaling om hun eigen schip te laten bouwen, een schip met woonruimte met voldoende comfort om een gezin te stichten. Francine zou daar bij helpen haar loon te sparen voor zover dat mogelijk was want Londen was geen goedkope stad en er waren veel afleidingen in de winkels om te kopen, speciaal als je een jonge vrouw bent.

Francine en Leine kregen een cultuurschok toen ze in Londen aankwamen, het was zo groot en onbezonnen. Francine vertelde me dat de brutaliteit van het stadsleven werd afgezwakt door de beleefdheid en manieren van het Engelse volk, erg beleefd, dus beleefd, maar nooit wisten ze waar men bij de Engelsen stond, hoe zij hun taal gebruikten zoals rook en spiegels vol subtiliteiten, eufemisme en idiomen. Zelden was het gesproken woord duidelijk of direct.

Voordat wij naar Australië emigreerden in 1961 had oma Francine het daar veel over Engelse normen en waarden. Zo vertelde ze dat de Nederlandse directheid in de communicatie met buitenlanders regelmatig zorgde voor misverstanden tussen de Zeeuwse meiden en de Engelsen. In de eerste fase van hun betrekking wantrouwde ze dat zeer beleefde spreken. Ze waren bang dat er een onaangename boodschap kan worden verborgen die ze niet kennen.

Heel aardig zijn kan het vermoeden wekken, in de gedachten van Nederlanders, dat iemand een speciale gunst nodig heeft. Beleefdheid kan ook irritatie veroorzaken omdat het als tijdverspilling wordt beschouwd. De Engelsen hielden van de Zeeuwse meisjes, maar vonden ze vreselijk direct. Ze noemden een vloek een vloek waarbij ze de juiste zelfstandige naamwoorden gebruikten om dingen te benoemen, geen eufemisme om een onaangename waarheid of uitdrukking te verbergen.

Hier waren ze in de Engelse hoofdstad het middelpunt van de sterkste macht ter wereld, zowel economisch als militair, alles was groot in vergelijking met Terneuzen of Amsterdam. Wat het gemeen had met Terneuzen was de internationale scheepvaart van over de hele wereld.

In Terneuzen werden ze soms ingehuurd om gastvrouwen te zijn op Koninklijke jachten zoals Koning Leopold's *"Alberta"* of Kaiser Wilhelm's *"SMY Hohenzollern II"* en zelfs de Russische tsaar Nicolaas II's Imperial Yacht, *"Standart"* toen deze jachten door de Terneuzen kanaal van Terneuzen naar Gent voeren. In Londen kregen ze de kansen niet om Koninklijke Prinsen en Prinsessen incognito te ontmoeten, maar in Terneuzen wel. Denk daar maar eens over zei tante Leine die mij later ook grote verhalen vertelde.

Terwijl ze aan het werk waren in het Ritz ontmoetten ze *Emmeline Pankhurst*, leider van het Britse Suffragette, en spraken ze over sociale onrechtvaardigheden. Emmeline stelde de Nederlandse meisjes voor aan een Virginia Stephen, die later romanschrijfster *Virginia Wolf* werd.

Francine zei dat ze zoveel gemeen hadden met de Engelse vrouwen, het enige dat haar dwarszat was het Engelse klassensysteem. Alles werd er op een soort snobistische, onmenselijke manier ondergebracht.

De meisjes van van Aalst waren arbeidersklasse.

Ze kregen van de Engelsen te horen op een toon en een manier die klonk alsof arbeiders klasse een ziekte of een aandoening was maar Francine wees dit af als onzin. Zij was nooit op haar tongetje gevallen. Ook keek ze naar een groter beeld dat van wat de toekomst voor vrouwen zou kunnen zijn. Uiteindelijk zei ze dat vrouwen verantwoordelijk waren voor hun eigen leven en geen slachtoffer of overtuiging mochten zijn en dat ze zich volledig moesten onderwerpen aan het gezag van de man, zoals geëist door conservatieve religieuzen. Maar Francine, net als Emily, geloofden sterk en streefden voor het stemrecht van vrouwen. Maar toch al voelde ze zichzelf als gelijkwaardig met mannen in elk aspect van het leven, inclusief sparen om een schip te kopen met Kees haar toekomstige echtgenoot.

Zeeuws-Vlaamse vrouwen waren niet zozeer ondergeschikt aan hun mannelijke tegenhangers, of ze nu aardappels raapten of suikerbieten steken of vlas spinnen in de spinnerijen. Vrouwen waren al gelijk aan mannen in termen van loon en status, en er waren ook niet te veel genderspecifieke banen. Een vrouw kon het zo goed doen als een man. Het bewijs hiervan was dat ze tenslotte geregeerd waren door twee Nederlandse koninginnen: Emma en Wilhelmina, de laatste koningin zou het grootste deel van Francines leven regeren.

Wilhelmina was niet veel ouder dan Francine, ze waren tijdgenoten.

Ze gingen graag naar shows aan de westkant van Londen waar ze het had over Oscar Wilde's *"The Importance of Being Ernest,"* dat was de eerste keer dat ik de naam *Oscar Wilde* hoorden. Ze hielden van Oscar, omdat hij alle vroomheid en schijnheiligheid van de vorige eeuw werd omgedraaid en de Victoriaanse geschiedenis en dubbele standaarden op een grappige en sarcastische manier werden blootgelegd.

De Victoriaanse samenleving was niet anders dan de *'verwaande beter wetende Ollanders'*, maar niet zoals in Terneuzen waar geen culturele klasse barrières te zien waren waarvan ze zich van bewust waren. Het leek dat in Terneuzen een soort maaiveld mentaliteit handhaafde, meest van de bevolking daar kende elkaar en grootdoenerij of verwaand zijn werd daar gewoon uitgelachen.

Als kind in de jaren vijftig vertelde tante Leine mij hoe ze in het gigantische reuzenrad van 1894 gingen voor de India-tentoonstelling in Londen, het was de grootste ter wereld en de kar waarin ze zaten had plaats voor 40 mensen en bleef wel twee uur hoog in de lucht hangen om dat er een van de motoren stuk was. Ze giechelde en zei dat de uitzichten fantastisch waren. Eén van de andere vijfentwintig passagiers waarmee ze vastzaten in de reuzenradwagen was een Nederlandse man genaamd Meneer Boot een scheepsbouwer van stalen schepen uit Nederland. Leine had nog steeds het bezoekkaartje van deze meneer Boot ze liet het mij zien het was geel van oudheid wel, 55 jaar oud zei ze. Een paar weken nadat ze uit de reuzenradsaga waren gered, op hun vrije dag, nodigden Francine en Leine de heer Boot uit voor thee of een Jonge Jenever (Nederlandse Bols Gin) in de *Ritz's très chic pre-dinnerdrinks lounge*. Vooral omdat ze Nederlands konden praten met hem en Francine hem kon horen over zijn scheepsbouw.

Meneer Boot vertelde hen dat hij in Engeland was om te leren van de Engelse en Schotse scheepsbouwtechnieken. Vooral de snelle Clipper-zeilschepen zoals de Cutty Stark, hoe snel en elegant ze zeilden in een recordtijd van 72 dagen van Melbourne Australië naar Londen. Meneer Boot's idee was om zulke snelle maar dan plat bodem stalen klipper-ontwerp bouwen voor de binnenwateren van Europa. Ze moesten klein genoeg zijn om in de soms veelal smalle waterwegen tegen de wind in te zigzaggen en ook genoeg tonnage hebben om het voor de schippers rendabel te maken. Meneer Boot wilde baanbrekend zijn met zijn nieuwe ontwerpen. Dit intrigerende gesprek met Meneer Boot zouden de vrouwen niet snel vergeten en met het oog op de toekomst zou dit later weer van pas komen.

Leine dacht dat de Londense warenhuizen een 'paradijs voor dames' waren. Een bezoek was meer een bestemming zoals een bezoek aan kunstgalerijen of musea of het strand. Ze waren veel meer dan alleen een grote en goed gevulde stadswinkel zoals in Terneuzen. Voor hen waren deze verbluffende nieuwe warenhuizen ontmoetingsplaatsen en af en toe lunchen ze daar met hun Engelse vriendinnen.

Francine schreef in een van haar brieven naar huis over de betoverende warenhuizen zoals *Selfridges, Harrods*. Deze hadden honderden afdelingen; restaurants, een daktuin, lees- en schrijfkamers, ontvangstruimtes voor buitenlandse bezoekers, een EHBO-kamer en, belangrijker nog, een klein leger van bekwame vriendelijke en knap uitziende assistenten die niet alleen dienden als gidsen voor deze winkelschat, maar ook grondig vermengd en gecharmeerd waren in de kunst van het verkopen.

*"Ja, je moet goed begrijpen"* zei Francine, "dat voor ons was het enkel maar etalage winkelen want wij werkten in London voor geld te sparen maar af en toe werd er wel gespendeerd, daar is toch het geld voor hé? iets om uit te geven, *anders heeft geld geen waarde*; knap mens dacht ik, trouwens dit soort nieuwe departement winkels was de verhoging van het consumentisme.

Ze bezochten het warenhuis Selfridges een week voordat ze terug zouden reizen naar Nederland om kleine, niet duur, maar wel indrukwekkende en passend voor de individueel voor wie het cadeautje was bestemd zoals hun broers en zussen en goede vrienden.

Ze kochten geschenken zoals met de handgemaakt fijne gehaakte zakdoekjes, kleine decoratieve flesjes parfum. Francine kocht voor haar aanstaande Kees een Engelse schipperstrui, een donker blauwe bijna zwarte wollen coltrui met knopen. De trui was het duurste van alle cadeautjes, ze zou niet beseffen dat dit cadeau twintig jaar lang bijna elke dag gedragen zou worden.

Na drie jaar was hun tijd in Engeland voorbij, ze pakten hun koffers, bewaarden hun herinneringen en oefenden nieuwe levensvaardigheden.

Zo reisden ze terug naar Terneuzen vol met levenservaring, klaar om hun toekomst verder op te bouwen en te beklimmen.

# HOOFDSTUK 2

*Trouwen, bouwen en kinderen.*

De Noordzee was woelig met een krachtige ijskoude November wind, de Van Aalst-zusjes Francine en Leine zeilden 's nachts vanuit Londen op dezelfde Raderstoomboot waarop ze 3 jaar eerder heen zeilden. Ze zaten in de verwarmde en gezellige deksalon en aten hete snert-erwtensoep en dronken hun warme chocolade melk met amandel gevulde koeken. Ze vroegen zich af wie ze af zouden komen halen bij terugkomst in Vlissingen. Ze hadden enkele weken geleden slechts één ansichtkaart naar hun ouders gestuurd met gegevens van de tijd van aankomst. Francine had een lange brief aan Kees geschreven, waarin zij hem niet alleen adviseerde van haar ontmoeting met meneer Boot, de scheepsbouwer, maar ook dat ze 300 gulden had gespaard. Misschien was dat wel een uitdaging voor Kees om zijn spaargeld te evenaren met het hare. Ook gaf zij een subtiele hint over huwelijksplannen, ze schreef dat die Engelse stads mannen niet te vergelijken waren met de stoere en forse lichaamsbouw van de Zeeuwse. Ze vond de meeste Engelsen stadsmannen maar dandies, tenminste dat schreef ze aan Kees.

Het terugkomstonthaal in Vlissingen was sensationeel, al haar 6 zussen en moeder waren in een spannende feeststemming wachtend in de Zeeland Steamboat Terminal overstelpt met bossen bloemen voor de aankomende van Aalst zusters alsof ze koninklijk waren. Kees en zijn broer Bram wachtten ook bescheiden op de achtergrond met trossen rozen. Francien en Leine leken wel een paar filmsterren uit Hollywood.

Alles fleurde op bij hun aankomst met alle tekenen van vreugdevolle hereniging. Tot ieders verbazing gaf Francine aan Kees geruststellende knuffels, en nog meer knuffels, strakke, strakke knuffels. Het kon haar niet schelen wat mensen van haar zouden denken.

Enkele dagen na de terugkeer van Francine en Leine uit Londen gingen ze beiden weer aan de slag als receptioniste in Hotel Rotterdam in Terneuzen. Kees begon met de hulp van zijn broer Bram te onderzoeken wat voor soort schip hij nodig zou hebben om een behoorlijke boterham te verdienen. Dit vereiste wat kritisch denken, niet alleen over efficiënte ontwerpen, maar ook over economie en concurrentie. Het moest een schip zijn dat bijna elk soort type vracht kon vervoeren en 40 jaar lang een comfortabel levenswijze voor heel de familie aan boord kon bieden.

Dinsdag 7 juni 1910 op het gemeentehuis van Terneuzen zijn Kees en Francine getrouwd. Zij hadden een burgerlijk huwelijk; Het is misschien goed om hier te vermelden dat Kees en Francine's toekomstige kinderen in geen enkele religie werden gedoopt. Ze vonden de kerk belangrijk voor mensen die geen filosofische reikwijdte hadden om richting te vinden over de verborgen levenspaden. De Paulusses en de van Aalsts waren Nederlandse liberalen uit de achttiende eeuw onder invloed van de verlichting van de zeventiende eeuw. Hun ideeën waren om de verschillen van mensen te respecteren. Ze waren lovenswaardige burgers en benadrukten respect voor alle culturen, religies en ideologieën en de grote uitspraak dat we onvoorwaardelijk van elkaar moeten houden. Het is te begrijpen hoe ze zich voelden, drie jaar afwezigheid zorgde ervoor dat het hart stichter wordt, maar ze zeggen ook uit het oog uit het hart, maar zo is het gelukkig niet verlopen. Leine zou in 1915 trouwen met de 27-jarige Schipper Abraham, beter bekend als Bram van Hanegem.

In 1959 vierden Francine en Kees hun vijftigste huwelijk. Ik als tien jarig ventje feliciteerden hen met één handschudding, omhelzingen (knuffels noemen ze dat nu he)en *kweet nie oe veel kussen*. Daar was Francine wel op gesteld en vond het fijn. Bij opa Kees bleef het met één hand en omhelzing maar er werd veel gelachen. En dat gelach, zei Francine, is het geheim om levenslang lief voor elkander te blijven. Ze onderdrukte het veel samen lachen en niet om je emoties te veel te intellectuelen om acceptatie nodig te hebben. En een groot deel van je acceptatie komt van lachen. Echtparen die niet samen om zichzelf kunnen lachen, accepteren hun relaties waarschijnlijk niet erg. Ze kunnen de unieke gebreken en onvermijdelijke struikelingen van de mensheid misschien niet tolereren, net zo min als ze hun eigen fouten kunnen verdragen.

Kees en Bram en zijn oudere broer Ko waren visionair geworden sinds ze in 1900 de *Parijse Expositie Universelle*, algemeen bekend als de Wereldtentoonstelling, bezochten. Ze hadden de trein in Terneuzen genomen die om 7 uur 's ochtends naar Parijs vertrok en daar om 4 uur' s middags arriveerden. Onmiddellijk bezochten ze de beroemde Eifeltoren om half 5 in de middag om te kijken en iets te leren van de nieuw geïnstalleerde *Otis hydraulische liften*. Ik moet hier constateren dat voor de meeste Nederlanders hun leven op de klok draait tot zenuwen toe, bijna elke minuut wordt bijgehouden.

Tien jaar later hadden ze het nog steeds over de toegangspoort, die 60.000 betalende bezoekers per uur toeliet. Ze waren nog vol ontzag voor alle nieuwe uitvindingen die ze zagen in het elektriciteitspaviljoen: Pratende foto's, elektrische trams en auto's, waaronder de nieuwe dieselmotoren, elektronische roltrappen, de telegrafoon (een magnetische audiorecorder)en röntgenapparatuur. In het Optiekpaleis zagen ze een indrukwekkende en zeer grote sterke lenzen van de telescopen waar zij door keken en goed duidelijk de oppervlakte van de maan in detail konden zien. Dan was er nog de rolband zijwandelingen, een voetpad maar dan met *hupsekee 1600 mensen tegelijk er op* net zoals op de nu transport loopbaan op Schiphol. Het liep langs al de paviljoens. Er waren toen in 1900 meer uitvindingen dan in het jaar 2020. Ja er is niets nieuws onder de zon zegt een oud spreekwoord en 'tis waar. De Paulusse broers woonden ook seminars bij over maritiem transport.

In hun onderzoek om een schip te laten bouwen waren ze zich bewust van snelle veranderingen in technologie, globalisering, elektronische communicatie, productie en massaconsumptie waaronder veranderingen in het sociale weefsel van de samenleving. De status van mannen en vrouwen werd snel gelijk. Vrouwen kregen formeel onderwijs en verdienden meestal hun eigen geld. Madame Marie Curie ontving samen met haar man in 1903 de helft van de Nobelprijs voor natuurkunde voor hun onderzoek naar de spontane radiumstralingen en fysica. Er waren in hun leven op dat moment zoveel uitvindingen waardoor de Paulusse broers serieuser gingen nadenken en over duurzaamheid die in de toekomst werd geprojecteerd. Een nieuwe wereld kreeg vorm die gevuld was met allerlei soorten experts, van wetenschappers, statisticus en ingenieurs. Ze waren zich er zeer van bewust dat het jaar 1900, het begin van de 20e eeuw, een tijdperk van enorme verandering was op bijna al de gebieden en vroegen zich af wat voor soort samenleving en economie er zouden ontstaan.

*De gebroeders Paulusse keerden opgewonden en hergebruikt terug van de 'Paris Exposition Universelle', de restanten van hun ervaring maakten hen jarenlang visionaire innovators, ondernemers en kritische denkers.*

Voor hun huwelijksreis reisden Kees en Francine naar de stad van Johannes Vermeer, Delft, waar ze logeerden bij een van Francines zusters die een alleenstaande moeder was maar die totale liefde en steun had van de familie van Aalst hoewel ze niet konden begrijpen waarom ze zou leven in *Olland* onder die alle eigenzinnige met zelfingenomen Hollanders. Maar Francine wist waarom, ze vertelde me dat de vader van haar kind een rijke kunsthandelaar in Delft was die getrouwd was met een Française, maar zei dat hij een eerbare fatsoenlijke man was en haar zus in een huis met twee verdiepingen onderhield. Ironisch, een paar kilometer vandaan Scheepsbouwbedrijf Boot en Zoonen.

De reis van Terneuzen naar Delft duurde bijna vier uur met boot, bus en trein zowel als paard en wagen. Ze reisden met een hoop geld in haar klein, fijn en Zeeuws ontworpen leder handtasje met de inhoud van 1500 guldens. Een klein fortuin dat zij en Kees hadden opgespaard. De families van Aalst en Paulusse, vrienden en kennissen hadden bijgedragen met wat flinke guldens. Zij konden dat doen. Dat kwam zo, er werden geen huwelijksgeschenken aan het echtpaar gegeven. In plaats daarvan stond er een erg mooi koperen geldkistje, gemaakt door Kees, blinkend gepoetst in het receptiecentre van Café De Vriendschap, vast geschroefd op een toonbank zodat niemand het kon jatten. Dat verhaal vond ik altijd avontuurlijk *het jatten van opa's geld kistje*. Wonderlijk vooral wat dat kistje meegemaakt heeft. Ik heb op de dag van vandaag dit prachtige koperen geldkistje nog het staat op een eere plaats in mijn woonkamer hier in Australië, zo mooi is het. Doordrenkt met gedurfd familiegeschiedenis. Bruiloftgasten deponeerden daar hun guldens in, Francine zei dat er wel twaalf gouden guldens in zaten. Er waren toevallig rijke lui bij, de redenaar Lensen, de Vermast Familie, de gebroeders Ribbens, allemaal vrienden van Kees en de Duitse Consulaat in Terneuzen zowel als de directeur van Hotel Rotterdam. *Dat was toch zoveel praktischer dan het ontvangen van "nutteloze spotgoedkope huwelijkscadeaus", vertelde Francine mij met een lachje.* Ik werd bewust dat veel families in Terneuzen hun middelen bundelen voor het collectieve goed om zaken te beginnen, zo konden veel binnenvaartschepen particulier worden gefinancierd.

De Scheepswerf van Boot en Zonen in Delft had een uitstekende reputatie voor het bouwen van sterke stalen en snel gladde ijzeren rivierklippers. Ze waren veelzijdige vrachtschepen, geschikt voor de Noordzeekustwateren en op de ondiepe kronkelde waterwegen van Europa. Deze rivierklippers hadden snelheid, waren goedkoop in gebruik zonder het milieu te schaden of de waterwegen te vervuilen door geen brandstof te gebruiken. Ze werden voortgestuwd door de wind die waaide in de zeer sterke zeilen gewoven van lokaal geteelde hennep in Zeeuws-Vlaanderen. Ze waren platbodems een voordeel voor reparatie en onderhoud, ze konden als het ware gewoon op de wadden bij Terneuzen geparkeerd worden en met hoog water weer drijven. Voor diepzeekustzeilen gebruikten ze verstelbare kielen, meestal *zwaarden* genoemd, die verlaagd zouden worden afhankelijk van de windkracht en waterdiepte waardoor de klipper meer stabiliteit en evenwicht zou krijgen en niet zou kapseizen. De afmetingen van Kees' en Francines schip bij de bouw was lengte 2800 cm met 569 cm en kan tot 174 ton vracht vervoeren.

Ze registreerden de thuishaven van hun schip in Terneuzen Zeeuws-Vlaanderen. De regio Terneuzen kende in 1910 zoals nu een dynamische snelle industriële groei. Veel Italianen, Fransen investeerden in de chemie, en de Belgen hadden een grote staalfabriek gebouwd. Voor de productie waren natuurlijke hulpbronnen nodig die vanuit alle hoeken van de aarde naar Terneuzen, Gent of Antwerpen werden verscheept. Boeren uit Zeeuws-Vlaanderen verbouwden in zeer grote mate vlas, suikerbieten en grote variëteiten van granen, aardappelen en heel veel uien waaronder ook bosproducten, zoals bomen die naar de Noord-Hollandse Bruynzeelse potlood- en fineerfabrieken moesten worden vervoerd.

Het schip van de toekomstige Paulusse moet honderden tonnen suikerbieten kunnen vervoeren voor de suikerfabrieken, of zand voor de glasfabrikanten of steenzout voor de grote chemische fabrieken. Grote stenen werden later vervoerd vanuit Duitsland en Scandinavië voor de versterking van de Zeeuwse dijken, zo als zand en grind gewonnen uit de grote zandbanken in de Schelde. Hier was inderdaad een dynamische toekomst.

Vaak moesten grote vrachtschepen die Terneuzen niet binnen konden komen en zo omdat ze te zwaar geladen waren om door het *kanaal Terneuzen Gent* te varen. Ze moesten dan gedeeltelijk worden gelost in kleine binnenschepen zoals de Scheldestroom, zodat ze de sluizen konden passeren en vervolgens konden lossen in opslagplaatsen langs het kanaal speciaal voor chemische producten, calciumijzererts, kolen, opslag van alle soorten graan en Steenzout voor de productie van nitraat en kunstmest voor de chemie- en cokesbedrijven. Allemaal direct gelegen aan het *kanaal van Gent naar Terneuzen.* Het overgrote deel van de producten wordt per schip vervoerd. Er was ook een bloeiende Textielindustrie die vlaswol exporteerde. Na veel onderzoek besloten Kees en Francine om de bestelling te plaatsen voor de bouw van hun schip.

Het was niet alleen de aanschaf van het schip, maar een schipper moest een goede manager zijn en een goede logistiekmedewerker, die berekende hoe lang een reis zou duren, afhankelijk van hoe gunstig de wind was, voor de wind of tegen de wind. De succesvolle schipper was een zeeman, maar moest ook functioneren als bekwaam zakenman en dan nog op de *wilde vaart* zonder vracht, beurs of controle maar met harde concurrentie.

Onder het roken van een grote Schimmelpenninck sigaar begroette Cornelis Boot hen met zeldzame hartelijkheid, hij moet hun geld hebben geroken, geld is altijd reden om minnelijk te zijn. Zijn gebruikelijke houding was meestal een strikt zakelijke feit met een calvinistische toon en een manier die niet gemakkelijk gegeven werd aan lichtzinnigheid of het subtiel kennen van diplomatie. Francine had alle harde zilveren- en gouden munten omgewisseld en haar damestasje zat nu propvol met papiergeld.

Cornelis Boot was een beetje geschrokken, het stond op zijn uiterlijk omdat het zelden voorkwam dat een Nederlandse vrouw met haar man meeging om een bestelling voor een schip te plaatsen.

De overeenkomsten werden getekend en de 1500 gulden die als aanbetaling op de onderhandelingstafel werd geplaatst waar een zenuwachtige assistent van Cornelis Boot het wel drie keer nauwkeurig telde. De totale kosten van de bouw van het schip bedroegen 6500 gulden, die over een periode van vijf jaar moesten worden afgelost tegen een rente van 4%. Een speciale verzekering werd ondertekend voor het geval van een economische neergang wanneer de winst zou afnemen. Het zou vier maanden in beslag nemen om de bouw van de éénmaster rivierklipper van 174 ton te voltooien.

De naam van het schip moet bijzonder zijn, het moet wat zeggen vonden Kees en Francine. Hun leven in Terneuzen draaide voor altijd rond de Schelde. Voor hen was de rivier met zijn uitmonding de Honte als een orkest, opgemaakt van natuurschoon, stromend water met speelse otters, zeehondjes en springende vissen. Voor hen was de Scheldslag het ritme van het leven. Hun werk en brood was te danken aan de commerciële en natuurlijke rijkdommen en kansen die de Schelde bood en ging bieden. Het vormde en duiden hun personages en persoonlijkheid. Het zorgde ervoor dat ze het verleden begrepen zoals de 360 km lange Schelde-stroom die naar de toekomst stroomde. De Scheldecultuur was overal te zien in gebeeldhouwde kunst en architectuur zoals *Schelde Gothic*, de vele muzikale thema's van de Schelde. In de schilderijen van niemand minder dan *Peter Paul Rubens, Jan van Eyck, Pieter Breugel* en *Jan Gossaert*. Ooit was Francine gastvrouw voor componist *Peter Benoit* die aan boord was van het Belgische Koninklijk Jacht *Prins Albert*, toen het Terneuzen bezocht. En zelfs de dichter *Jan Hammenecker*,1878-1932, had dit gedicht voorgedragen op één van de verjaardagsfeestjes van de meisjes van Aalst;

*'Zolang ik ademloos spreek met ontvoerde taal, zal*
*ik over jou spreken, mijn Schelde-stroming.'*

Het was niet meer dan normaal dat hun schip als *Scheldestroom* werd gedoopt ... een stroom naar de toekomst.

Ik hoorde vaak de verhalen hoe een schipper, na de ondertekening van de contracten, de Hennep touwfabrieken en de Hennep teeltvelden van zeilfabrikanten bezocht. De vezel van de planten werd gebruikt voor alle touwwerken en voor de productie van zeilen die op de Scheldestroom allemaal waren gemaakt van Hennep. Hennepvezel was onmisbaar bij de bouw en navigatie van zeilschepen, die een grote behoefte hadden aan touwwerk, canvas en kitmateriaal. Dit omvatte de tuigage en de scheepskabels. Hennep was na hout het meest gebruikte materiaal voor de scheepsbouw. Geen enkele andere natuurlijke vezel is zo bestand tegen de krachten van de open zee en de werking van zout water. Er waren grote hennepboerderijen in Zuid-Holland in de buurt van de scheepswerf. Zeemanskleding en uitrusting voor nat weer werd vaak gemaakt van hennep en de kapitein hield zijn logboek bij op henneppapier. Met hennepolielampen kon de bemanning benedendeks lezen in de Bijbel (gedrukt op henneppapier). Om schipbreuk te overleven en ervoor te zorgen dat er voedsel aan boord was, hielden schepen een voorraad hennepzaad aan. De grote industriële teelt in Nederland was rond 1915 beëindigd, afgezien van enkele kleinere culturen voor lokaal gebruik.

In 1968 vertelde Opa Kees me dat hij en zijn vrienden soms hennep rookten vermengd met pijptabak en dat er geen poespas werd gemaakt. Het kwam niet op bij de mensen met een gezond intelligent verstand om het te verbieden. Trouwens, alcohol was de vijand van de gemeenschap. Niet Hennep. Hij had zijn kleinzoons, waaronder mijzelf ontmoedigd en verzekerde hij me dat hij nooit veel rookte en dronk zelden. Ik geloofde hem omdat we in datzelfde jaar een tweedaagse fietstocht maakten langs de Zeeuws-Vlaamse waterwegen, op 85-jarige leeftijd trapte hij nog flink door op de fiets en als 19-jarige had ik moeite hem bij te houden. De Gouden Eeuw van Nederland zou niet zonder hennep hebben plaatsgevonden zei opa en dat blijkt de waarheid want Google zegt het ook.

Het eerste meisje werd begin maart 1911 geboren. Voor die geboorte was Francine naar het huis van haar moeder gegaan om haar dochtertje Elisabeth Janna Paulusse te baren. Ze noemden haar *kleine Bette,* een gezonde baby van 3,4 kg. Ik weet dit, omdat Francine aanwezig was bij de geboorte van mijn zus Marianne in 1961 en ik hoor haar nog steeds zeggen: "Oh, wat is dat een mooi gewicht hetzelfde als kleine Bette". Eén van de redenen waarom Francine niet aan boord beviel, was dat Kees een lucratief contract had gesloten om stenen te vervoeren en extra dekhanden aan boord nodig had om stenen te laden en te lossen, waardoor er geen ruimte was voor Francine en de kleine Bette noch Leine die in de zorg zou helpen met kleine Bette.

Van februari tot november 1911 voer de Scheldestroom de Nederlandse binnenvaart rivieren waar veel steenbakfabrieken aan lagen. De beschikbaarheid van klei en brandstof was belangrijk voor steenfabrieken zodat veel steenfabrieken zich vestigden in kleigebieden of aan de rand daarvan. De Scheldestroom lag langs de getijdenrivier de *Hollandsche IJssel* waarvan de oevers worden gedomineerd door vele verschillende types steenfabrieken. Gele ijzeren bakstenen uit het rivier gebaggerde slib werden gebakken in veldsteenovens. De ovens werden gestookt met turf uit de veengronden uit het achterland van Haastrecht tot IJsselmonde. Er waren zo'n 40 steenfabrieken met in totaal zo'n 100 veldsteenovens. Langs alle grote Nederlandse delta riviersystemen is rivierklei aanwezig en vroeger werden de gebakken stenen per schip naar klanten vervoerd.

Op een zeer koude zaterdag, 16 december 1911, beviel Francine van haar tweede kind. Een zoontje, ze noemden hem *Jan Pieter Paulusse*. Hij werd geboren aan boord van De Scheldestroom, afgeleverd door een mannelijke verloskundige in aanwezigheid van een vrouwelijke verloskundige. Die dag was de Scheldestroom gestrand op de zandbank net buiten Terneuzen. Dit was geen ramp voor platbodems maar wel een lastige situatie. Francine voelde, onverwachts, en te vroeg, dat de weeën van de naderende bevalling plotseling begonnen en ze vreesde complicaties, Kees stapte in zijn roeiboot en gebaarde een passerend Tjalk om de verloskundige te bellen toen ze de sluis bereikten. Er was een buitens telefoon aan een paal waar men voor eerste hulp bij ongelukken kon bellen. Binnen een uur kwamen twee verloskundigen aan op een snelle diesel medische reddingsboot zal ik maar zeggen. De mannelijke verloskundige had een opleiding in verloskunde en de vroedvrouw was alleen goed voor gemakkelijke bevallingen zonder complicaties. *Jan Pieter Paulusse* arriveerde blij en gelukkig zonder enige complicaties. Het was een makkelijke bevalling, vertelde Francine mij, een "stukje cake". Zijn wieg werd onder de kerstboom gelegd in de warme gezellige roef. Kees verheugde zich bij de geboorte van een jongen dat was een toekomstige matroos. In 1911 werd 60% van alle baby's thuis afgeleverd door verloskundigen en de andere 30% thuis door mannelijke verloskundigen en slechts 10% in ziekenhuizen. Kees betaalde de mannelijke verloskundige zes gulden en de vrouwelijke verloskundige 5 gulden, de dieselsnelheidsboot kostte nog eens 9 gulden, allemaal contant betaalt.

Francines zuster, Jane, kwam uit Delft om te blijven zolang het nodig was om te koken en de baby te verwennen en Kees' broer, Ko, kwam helpen als matroos. Een taak die eerder door Francine was gedaan. Jane en Ko bleven aan boord zolang als het nodig was totdat de baby, Jan Pieter, en Francine het alleen afkonden.

Francine had een gouden koord om haar boog. Ze was een fantastische kokkin, daarom noemde ik haar dikwijls "Oma Chef". Niets was pakketvoeding of gefabriceerd voedsel.

In haar dag waren er geen koelkasten aan boord, die waren toen heel duur en te luxe. En "'t was eigenlijk niet nodig", vond Francine. Al het vlees werd gerookt of in grote stenen potten gedaan. De gefrituurde schnitzels en spekjes bleven in hun eigen vet bewaard in stenen potten. Ze kochten groente en fruit goedkoop. In tijden van overvloed maakte ze heel gezonde zuurkool en kweekte die in grote Keulse potten. Ze steriliseerde groenten en fruit genoeg om er wel vier maanden van toe te komen. Ze bakte al haar eigen broodsoorten..

# HOOFDSTUK 3



*Oorlog 1914- 1918*
*De stroom vluchtelingen was eindeloos en al snel waren*
*alle grensdorpen van Zeeuws-Vlaanderen vol.*

Op dinsdag 28 juli begon de Eerste Wereldoorlog en op vrijdag 31 juli 1914 werden 200.000 jonge Nederlandse mannen gemobiliseerd en opgeroepen voor militaire dienst. Op 4 augustus 1914 staken Duitse troepen de grens met België over, waardoor de twee matrozen van de Scheldestroom moesten toetreden tot het leger. De verwijdering van zoveel mannen uit de beroepsbevolking en de neutraliteit van Nederland had een vrijwel onmiddellijk economisch effect omdat de economie afhankelijk was van de export en import van natuurlijke hulpbronnen uit de koloniën.

De Eerste Wereldoorlog heeft de binnenvaart dan ook hard getroffen doordat alle vormen van binnenlandse- en internationale transporten plotseling afnamen of erger nog tot stilstand kwamen. Door het ontbreken van sociale zekerheidsvoorzieningen kwamen individuele schippers vrijwel onmiddellijk in ernstige moeilijkheden.

Kees en Francine hadden het geluk dat ze in juni 1914 hun laatste hypotheekschuld van de Scheldestroom aflosten. Een ander geluk was dat ze in Zeeuws Vlaanderen zaten waar duizenden Belgische vluchtelingen een reddende toevlucht zochten. Twintigduizend militairen van het Nederlandse leger bewaakten de Nederlandse Belgische grenzen in

Zeeuws Vlaanderen alleen. Al deze mensen hadden vervoer en voeding nodig.

Motorolie was gerantsoeneerd en bij gebrek aan aanbod was het een concurrentievoordeel dat de Scheldestroom geen gebruik maakte van brandstof, daar voor, en het feit dat Kees en Francien hulpzaam en hartelijke mensen waren, was er veel vraag voor de diensten van de Scheldestroom.

Elders in Nederland werd voedsel gerantsoeneerd, maar niet in Zeeuws-Vlaanderen. Boeren waren daar de meest efficiënte landbouwproducenten van het land, wat betekende dat de Scheldestroom volgeboekt was voor vrachtvervoer van aardappelen, suikerbieten, tarwe en andere soort granen en uien naar de grote steden in het noorden van Nederland. De Duitse bezetters van België hadden zand en grind nodig, zo zeiden ze, om de beschadigde wegen en huizen in België te herstellen. Opnieuw was de Scheldestroom druk bezig met zand en grind dat direct in het ruim van de Scheldestroom gepompt werd van de zandbanken in de Wester Schelde, en voer het rechtstreeks naar Zee Brugge via de Noordzee met de zegeningen en bescherming van de oorlogse partijen.

De Eerste Wereldoorlog was voor veel Nederlanders een verkapte zegen en er werd veel geld verdiend door voedsel tegen hoge prijzen te verkopen met weinig overheidscontrole. Ongeveer het enige was een tekort aan mankracht.

Kees telde zijn zegeningen omdat Francine pas als dekhand kon fungeren nadat hij had afgesproken haar te helpen met de huishoudelijke taken. Inmiddels hadden ze twee kinderen, Bette, Jan-Pieter en er was een verdrietig miskraam. Jane, Francine's ongehuwde zus uit Delft en haar jonge peuter Evert waren naar Zeeland gekomen om Francine te helpen met de kinderen. Ze waren dankbaar voor hun grote en gezellige Roef waar 9 mensen comfortabel konden wonen.

Maar het waren zeer woelige tijden van angst, ieder moment kon Nederland worden aangevallen door Engelse en Duitse machten. Of je schip kon op een mijn lopen die gestrooid waren door de Duitsers en de Engelsen.

Er werd een gemeenschapsoproep gedaan naar de inwoners van Terneuzen om de duizenden Belgische vluchtelingen te helpen die Zeeuws-Vlaanderen binnenstroomden net zoals de vloed van Noah, wat gemakkelijk te doen is omdat de grenzen met België slechts een formaliteit waren en zeer doorlaatbaar. Kees zei dat er weinig of geen hulp was van de Nederlandse regering voor de eerste megagolven van vluchtelingen. Dit was omdat Nederland zich aan een strikte neutraliteit wou houden, hoewel de regering gedwongen werd in te grijpen toen het aantal vluchtelingen boven de miljoen uitkwam.

Toen ik hem voor het laatst sprak in 1968 vroeg ik mijn opa hoe in de dagen van 1914 men zo snel informatie kreeg en gehoor gaven omdat binnen een dag meer dan honderd vrijwilligers in Terneuzen zich aanmeldden om te dienen en opzetten van het vluchtelingenkamp te Hontenisse. Liefdadigheidsorganisaties en boeren reageerden ook zeer vlug binnen een periode van 24 uur, met voedseldonaties. Hij zei," Het Postkantoor in Terneuzen en omstreken had veel telegram-jongens in dienst, waaronder Francine's broers Piet en Hendrik en bovendien hadden we de nieuwste Marconi Morse-technologie die de zeeschepen van de wereld bediende vanuit het nieuwe Post-en Telegraafkantoor op de hoek van de Nieuwstraat en Kolkstraat gelegen pal naast de zeesluizen van het Terneuzen Gent kanaal. En voor de gewone burger was de communicatie ook goed die konden naar overal ter wereld telegrammen versturen en signalen ontvangen zonder kabels zoals elektromagnetische inductie. Zo kon men binnen een paar minuten elektronisch iets naar Nederlands-Indië en de VS of Zuid-Afrika sturen. Het gebeurde dikwijls dat hij een telegram kreeg waarop stond hoe laat een groot schip zou arriveren om van haar lading te worden gelicht en in welke haven de Scheldestroom naar toe moest varen voor de vrachtuitwisseling.

Op de Scheldestroom gebruikte men een vlagcode, en een misthoorncode die berichten doorgaf in tijden van nood. Kees met andere schippers experimenteerden met morsecodes en elektronisch seinlicht lang voordat Landstrijdkrachten innovatief op communicatie gebied werden, aldus dat zeiden de Nederlandse Marinemannen die vaak met Kees spraken en zijn hulp vroegen als er geen loodsen waren op de Schelde.

Hij zei dat in die tijd mensen behoorden tot gemeenschappen en verenigingen die daardoor dicht met elkaar verbonden waren. *Ik dacht in mijzelf het was niet zoals vandaag dat je je buurman niet kent maar iemand die een halve wereld van je weg is wel kent.* Opa ging voort met vertellen; "de meeste burgers waren lid van kerken, sportclubs of behoorden tot culturele verenigingen, bibliotheken", en hij zei dat snelle communicatie van lokale of wereldgebeurtenissen snel werd doorgegeven van mond tot mond. Mensen waren net een kettingreactie van communicatie, "je hebt gemerkt" zei hij "dat oudere mannen zich gezellig in kleine groepjes rond het kanaal op zitbanken zitten die speciaal geplaatst zijn rond bruggen, in de bosparken en in de winkelstraten. Mannen pratend en veel pratend en maar tabak kauwen en spugen en te kletsen over het alledaagse en over wie of wat dat voor hen passeert op dat moment *People watching*, noemen wij dat hier in Australië. Ik doe het ook erg graag als ik op een terrasje zit. Het is interessant en je lacht en leert als je het doet.

Dan, opa Kees ging vooruit op mijn stellende vraag over communicatie in 1914; waren er natuurlijk de kinderen op school. Ook zij waren gewend om belangrijke boodschappen door te geven aan Jan en alleman. Ook de kleine kruidenierswinkeltjes rond Terneuzen waarvan sommige al een telefoon hadden zodat er snel berichten naar de klanten konden worden overgedragen. Huisvrouwen in Terneuzen kwamen overdag in kleine groepjes bijeen en kletsten meerdere keren per dag met hun buren terwijl ze hun schone voetpaden zorgvuldig schrobden met een platte zeug.

*Ik dacht, er was toen een constante menselijke connectie, een echte sociale media, niet zoals vandaag, wanneer miljoenen zich geïsoleerd voelen van fysieke menselijke aanraking, gestrest en daardoor angstig raken. Vooral wanneer ze met gebogen hoofden hun telefoon blijkbaar aanbidden en terstond een antwoord verwachten uit het ether.*

In 1914 vloog het nieuws dus zeer snel van mond tot mond, elektronisch telegrammen en verbinding dat een tonende drong en een urgentie had op de emoties van de mensen. Het zal wel zo geweest zijn want over een honderd vrijwilligers reageerden positief op de gemeentelijke oproep.

Vijf van de zusters van Aalst en hun jonge broer Hendrik hielpen vrijwillig bij het opzetten van het vluchtelingenkamp in Hontenisse, geen gemakkelijke taak, zeker niet als het regende en nat was om tenten op te zetten en om in te slapen. Alles bleek koud en dampig. Ook de keukens, ziekenboeg, latrines en voedselvoorraden.

Iedereen ging aan boord van de Scheldestroom in Terneuzen waar het ook werd geladen met donaties van de burgerij zoals kleding, dekens, zeep en watercontainers. Terneuzens bakkers gaven brood, meel, gist, suiker en blikken thee. En de brandweer leende een waterzuiveringsinstallatie dat ook aan boord van de Scheldestroom geladen werd.

Onder gunstige wind zette de Scheldestroom koers naar Walsoorden, de haven van de gemeente Hontenisse. Aan boord waren ook vier lokale katholieke priesters en twee protestantse predikanten. Hun kerken waren zeer liberaal geweest in het verzamelen van voorraden. Het Ziekenhuis van Terneuzen schonk twee verpleegkundigen en een arts die ook plaats namen aan boord, ze zaten dan wel allemaal gezellig in de Roef. Zij werden vermaakt door de van Aalst zusters en dronken gezellig koffie, wat belangrijk was om een goede stemming op te wekken en de zenuwen te kalmeren.

Eén van de laadruimen van de Scheldestroom werd omgebouwd tot slaap- en rustruimte voor alle van Aalst-vrouwen en andere vrijwilligers, terwijl Francine, Kees en Jane in de Roef sliepen.

Alle vrijwilligers op de Scheldestroom kregen een fiets van een fietsenmaker in Terneuzen om samen naar het Vluchtelingenkamp te fietsen. Het zwaardere gereedschap werd per paard en wagen naar Hontenisse toegebracht, het was maar een paar kilometer van de haven van Walsoorden.

Francine vertelde ons veel verhalen over deze getraumatiseerde vluchtelingen ... in het kamp werden de vluchtelingen gesorteerd op basis van hun middelen. Er waren drie groepen: de rijken, de middenklasse en de armen die niets anders hadden dan de kleren op hun rug. De eerste twee groepen moesten betalen naar hun middelen, de derde groep hoefde niet te betalen. Elk vluchtelingengezin ontving na beoordeling een hulp noodgeval pakket bij aankomst.

Na enkele weken van het kamp opzetten en het organiseren van routines voor de vluchtelingen, functioneerde het kamp volledig. De Nederlandse regering had 20.000 Nederlandse militairen gemobiliseerd in Zeeuws-Vlaanderen, genoeg manschappen om de functies van kamp Hontenisse over te nemen. Onder de vluchtelingen in Hontenisse bevonden zich ook veel Belgische, Duitse en Engelse militairen. Kees zei dat er genoeg reden was voor het Nederlandse leger om het over te nemen.De van Aalst meiden en andere vrijwilligers keerden op het nippertje terug naar Terneuzen toen ontdekt werd dat zeer veel vluchtelingen besmet waren met de tyfuskoorts, een ernstige bacteriële infectie die wordt verspreid door parasieten. Iedereen in het vluchtelingenkamp was verplicht mondkapjes te dragen, handen te wassen en te hoesten in hun elleboog, dat had ik al eens eerder gehoord.

De stroom vluchtelingen was eindeloos en al snel waren alle grensdorpen van Zeeuws-Vlaanderen vol. Scholen en kerken werden omgebouwd tot opvangcentra. Privé-accommodatie stopte al snel. Toen er de tyfus uitbrak werd het verboden voor vluchtelingen om bij burgers ondergebracht te worden. Toen moest iedere vluchteling naar een kamp of dergelijke instantie waar enkel vluchtelingen toegang kregen.

# HOOFDSTUK 4

## Het vervoer van buitenlandse geïnterneerde militairen

Engelse jongens leken zo verloren en verbijsterd en leeg, ze konden niet geloven dat het machtige Engeland op dat moment verslagen was.

Hij wa s altijd bang was dat de Engelsen, Duitsers of de Amerikanen zijn schip op volle zee zouden stelen.

Francine nam het stuur over en Kees stelde de zeilen om de volle wind snelheid te krijgen. De race begon.

Kees kon zich niet herinneren hoeveel vliegtuigen hij van Cadzand met de Scheldestroom had vervoerd.

En ze zongen Sarie Marais - *Gelukkig zijn we de Britten kwijtgeraakt het was net als goede muziek toen het geluid van hun motor wegvaagde. Ze konden ons schip niet meer zien en we glipten weg in de stilte over de schelde zandbanken*

Het vervoer van buitenlandse geïnterneerde militairen. De First Royal Navy Brigade bestaande uit 1500 man en gestationeerd in Antwerpen, op aandringen van Winston Churchill de First Lord of the Admiralty. Toen de Eerste Wereldoorlog uitbrak werd deze Britse Brigade ingezet bij de verdediging van Antwerpen omdat het reguliere Belgische leger bijna was gedecimeerd. Op 17 oktober 1914 ging Antwerpen verloren door een felle Duitse aanval. Voor de controle over deze vitale haven werden de Britten onder de voet gelopen en moesten ze vluchten naar Zeeuws-Vlaanderen toen ze de Nederlandse grens overstaken en werden ze onmiddellijk geïnterneerd.

Kees had ervaring uit de eerste hand omdat de Scheldestroom werd gebruikt om veel van deze Britse jongens naar het vluchtelingenkamp Hontenisse en later nog naar Amersfoort en elders te vervoeren. Hontenisse was gelegen ten midden van een groot agrarische boerengemeenschap dat niet zo Engels gezind was vanwege de Boeren Oorlog. Hij vond het zielig en zei; "die Engelse jongens leken zo verloren en verbijsterd en leeg, ze konden niet geloven dat het machtige Engeland op dat moment verslagen was.

Maar hij ging verder, "wat voor deze Britten vervelend bleek te zijn, was dat Nederlandse boeren, net als de Zuid-Afrikaanse boeren, niet zo van de Engelsen hielden en de Britse jongens voelden dit enorm.

Dat kwam nog door de bijna kersverse herinnering over het vermeende onrecht dat de Boeren in Zuid-Afrika werd aangedaan met name het doden van tienduizenden Boerenmannen en -vrouwen en -kinderen van wie er meer dan 20.000 omkwamen in deze Britse zogenaamde concentratie kampen. "Ja", zei Kees. *Het hing altijd nog in het collectieve Nederlands geheugen ookal was het 13 jaar geleden.*" Kees zei, "zoiets mogen we nooit vergeten, en die Churchill samen met Lord Kitchener waren daar voorstanders van. Je weet dat je grootmoeder Francine bijna als dienstmeisje bij die Lord Kitchener ging dienen toen ze in Londen werkten, samen met Leine."

"Maak je geen zorgen", zei de Nederlandse kampcommandant in zijn toespraak aan de Engelse geïnterneerde militairen, "wij Nederlanders zullen jullie nooit behandelen zoals je onze neven en nichten behandelde in die vreselijke Britse concentratiekampen die jullie bouwden in Zuid Afrika. Hier in Nederland word je met respect en fatsoen behandeld". De meest populaire liedjes in die tijd waren de Boerenoorlogliederen

*Sari Marais, Bobbejaan Beklimt die Berg"*. Ze werden overal nog gezongen speciaal door Nederlandse militairen als ze marcheerden door het Zeeuws-Vlaamse Landschap. Maar de Britten zoals de Duitsers, Franse en Belgische troepen werden allemaal met formeel respect en houding ontvangen volgens de internationale regels van neutrale landen.

"Onze meiden", zei Kees, "Francine en Leine en met andere vrienden uit Terneuzen, die ook goed Engels, spraken waren weer als vrijwilliger naar Hontenisse vertrokken om de Engelse Navy boys te ontvangen en om te helpen met het papierwerk. Alles werd zorgvuldig opgeschreven zoals Jantje precies. Ik moet hier vertellen dat Francien een soort van "pen pal" vriendschap er op na hield met drie Engelse jongens die hun moeder erg misten. Ik kan de namen nog goed herinneren. Het waren George, James en Stuart.

De Eerste Wereldoorlog was in grote mate een economische zegen voor zeilboten eigenaars zoals Kees, vooral in een tijd van brandstoftekorten ... zo konden ze op prijs concurreren omdat ze niet hoefden te betalen voor gerantsoeneerde brandstof. Ten tweede was dat de Scheldestroom een snel zeilend schip was en werd gebruikt om Belgische vluchtelingen te zoeken die tevergeefs hadden geprobeerd om hun door oorlog geteisterde land te ontvluchten met kleine niet zeewaardige boten.

Alle Nederlandse schippers werden getroffen door de oorlog buiten hun grens: de handel werd verstoord, schepen gingen verloren, in beslag genomen door de Amerikanen en Engelsen en Duitsers en waren voedsel- en grondstoffen schaarste en de druk en eisen van de oorlogvoerende buren moesten worden verdragen om oorlog te voorkomen.

Hij vertelde het me in 1968, toen ik als 19-jarige hem zes maanden bezocht, we sprakten veel. Dat hij altijd bang was dat de Engelsen, Duitsers of de Amerikanen zijn schip op volle zee zouden stelen tijdens de Eerste Wereldoorlog 1914 – 1918. Het betekende altijd snel varen, optimaal gebruik maken van de wind en vooruit plannen en verstandig handelen. Het was een echte schok dat de Amerikaanse regering in één nacht 200 Nederlandse schepen in één keer in beslag had genomen, inclusief grote passagiersschepen zoals de *SS Rijndam* en de modernste schepen van de Nederlandse koopvaardijvloot, de grootste vrachtschepen in de wereld. Dit druiste in tegen de neutraliteit van Nederland wiens relatie, met de VS in ieder geval, verdeeld was. De voormalige President van de VS Teddy Roosevelt had in geheime gesprekken met de Duitser, Grand Admiral Alfred von Tirpitz en Keizer Wilhelm II gezegd om Nederland te veroveren en op te nemen in het grotere Duitse rijk. Daar kreeg koningin Wilhelmina lucht van en de hel barstte los.

De Engelsen deden hetzelfde, Kees maakte zich zorgen omdat hij af en toe de Scheldestroom op internationale wateren op de Noordzee moest bevaren wat buitengewoon gevaarlijk was omdat de Engelsen en Duitsers de Noordzee met zeemijnen hebben gezaaid ... het drijvende type meestal.

Wel tien keer zijn wij uitgevaren om voor Belgische drenkelingen te zoeken en een keer waren we zelf er bijna aan geweest, het kwam zo; Tijdens het oppikken van verdrinkende vluchtelingen langs de Noordzeekust in Nederlandse wateren onder de kust van Cadzand, zette een snelle mijnenveger van de Britse Royal Navy een achtervolging in op de Scheldestroom. Met een niet geringe trots vertelde Kees, "dat we ze op snelheid en wendbaarheid hadden verslagen. Gelukkig waren er maar vier Belgen aan boort en we hadden geen lading. Dit gaf een snelheidsvoordeel en we wisten waar de verraderlijke zandbanken waren en de Britten wisten dat niet. Zij hadden natuurlijk geen loods aan boord, wij hadden geen loodsen nodig omdat wij de Scheldemonding kenden zoals onze handpalm." Kees zei dat hij probeerde over de zandbanken te zeilen wat de Britten niet konden met hun zware mijnenveger en het zou een ramp voor hun zijn wanneer ze het probeerden. Afijn, Francine nam het stuur over en ik stelde de zeilen om de volle wind snelheid te krijgen. De race begon. Zeilen met de mijnenveger nastrevend, toen viel er plotseling een advectiemist. Dat is een soort mist die ontstaat wanneer er warme lucht in contact komt met het koude water. Het gebeurt of er nou wind zit of niet.

*Gelukkig zijn we de Britten kwijtgeraakt het was net als goede muziek toen het geluid van hun motor wegvaagde. Ze konden ons schip niet meer zien en we glipten weg in de stilte over de zandbanken. Als ik een religieus man was, zou ik zeggen dat de adem van God ons redde van de illegale kaping door de Britse marine.*

De ironie was natuurlijk dat er destijds duizenden Britse militairen in Nederlandse interneringskampen zeer goed werden verzorgd alsof ze onze eigen kinderen waren.

Op een andere keer vertelde hij mij dat hij via Vlissingen en Cadzand zo ver zuidelijk was gevaren naar Oostende, ZeeBrugge onder de Noordzeekust om verdrinkende vluchtelingen op te halen. Aan boord van de Scheldestroom bevonden zich ook personeel van de Nederlandse marine dat kennis nam van de afschuwelijke mijnen die de Duitsers en Engelsen langs de Nederlandse kust deponeerden.

Hun kinderen Bette en Jan-Pieter, zo jong als ze waren en tot hun grote vreugde, konden eerder een drijvende mijn zien dan de 'grootte mensen'.

Een van de meest opwindende genoegens, als ze inderdaad genoegens konden zijn in de oorlog, was om Britse, Franse en Duitse vliegtuigen te zien landen op het strand van Cadzand, gelegen op slechts 52 km van het oorlogsfront van Ieper, Passendale, en Broodeinde en de Somme rivier in noord Frankrijk. Daar was voortdurend zwaar vechten. Voor jaren hoorden men in Zeeuws Vlaanderen het verwoestende donder van het verre kanonvuur. Het veroorzaakte een bijna constante geluidstrilling.

Kees kon zich niet herinneren hoeveel vliegtuigen hij van Cadzand met de Scheldestroom had vervoerd. In zijn lading manifesto staat vermeld enkele van de soorten vliegtuigen zoals Bristol Type 22 - Britse tweezitsjager een Fokker Eindecker en een Siemen-Schuckert single Seat German Fighter-vliegtuig en een Frans Nieuport-verkenningsvliegtuig, die hij zich herinnerde dat hij op zijn schip droeg.

Maar de prijs was de noodlanding op Cadsand van een Britse DeO / 400-long range Britse bommenwerper die Sluis, Sas van Gent, Goes, Vlissingen en Zierikzee had gebombardeerd per ongeluk natuurlijk. Ook schepen probeerden ze te bombarderen, ze zagen ze voor Duitse schepen aan. De Britten ontkenden altijd dat ze dit en dat per ongeluk hadden gebombardeerd, maar uiteindelijk betaalden ze compensatie, maar het werd allemaal heel stil gehouden.

Oma Francine had vaak een gesprek met de piloten voordat zij werden geïnterneerd. Ik vroeg aan haar of ze dacht dat de piloten deserteurs waren, of dat het een echte noodlanding was. Ze antwoordde en zei: "Natuurlijk een noodlanding", daarna viel er een moment stil en zei ze: "arme moeders van deze jonge knappe intelligente Duitse en Engelse jongens… en oh ja één was een Australische piloot maar hij had zijn op de Scheldestroom werden vervoerd naar een Nederlandse vliegbasis waar ze aan de Nederlandse luchtmacht zouden worden toegevoegd.

# HOOFDSTUK 5



*De wilde jaren twintig*

De Grote Oorlog was voorbij de "roaring twenties begon.

De boog die de moderne wereld op haar weg van zelfvernietiging wierp, was de Grote Oorlog van 1914 -18. Het werd groot genoemd vanwege zijn omvang in plaats van vanwege enige opmerkelijke verdienste. Toen het vervolg in 1941 uitbrak, werd het eerdere conflict omgedoopt tot Eerste Wereldoorlog ter ere van de tweede.

De roaring twenties noemden ze het, de tijd van koortsachtige verandering, fenomenale rijkdom, decadentie en losse vrouwen. Het Nederlandse etablissement was geschokt door vrouwen die hun haar kort hadden afgeknipt, maar Francine niet. Ze had altijd kortgeknipt haar gehad, net als alle van Aalst-zusjes die de roedel ver voor waren. Toch was hun leven niet waanzinnig in de maalstroom die werd bestuurd door orkesten die 'het ritme van de 1920 bepaalden', bekend als de interbellumjaren die de droefheid en suggestiviteit van de nieuwe deuntjes samenvatten. Het was een tijdperk waarin amerikanisme de Nederlandse cultuur binnendrong en men was bang dat dit een identiteitscrisis zou kunnen veroorzaken, tot grote ergernis van de kerken en de heersende conservatieve regering. Maar Kees en Francine waren bezig een jong gezin voort te brengen en stoorden zich niet zo aan al de niet belangrijke fratsen van de tijd, in ieder geval zo leek het.

De zon scheen helder op een onbewolkte perfecte dag op de laatste dinsdag van de maand, 30 september 1924. Schipper Cornelis Paulusse, mijn opa [genoemd Kees voor kort], haastte zich opgewonden en met grote passen, zijn zwarte klompen kletterend op de geplaveide stenen terwijl hij op weg was naar het stadhuis van Terneuzen, om de geboorte van het vierde kind en de tweede zoon van zijn en jonge vrouw Francine te melden. Het stadhuis was de plek om geboorten en sterfgevallen te registreren. Uit de annalen van de familie Paulusse blijkt dat ze deze loop over de geplaveide stenen begon in 1594, het jaar waarin het stadhuis werd gebouwd nadat prins Willem van Oranje stadsrechten had verleend. 'Hoe heet je nieuwe zoon?' vroeg meneer Huizinga de griffier aan Kees. 'Zijn naam is Pieter Paulusse, we zullen hem Piet noemen.' Daarop werd de handtekening van Kees als informant geplaatst. Zoals de gewoonte was kregen alle vriendelijke ambtenaren van het stadhuis een sigaar van goede kwaliteit, geen goedkope rotzooi. Er werden felicitaties uitgesproken en de vrouwelijke ambtenaren ontvingen een doos met Belgische chocolaatjes die Francine twee dagen geleden had gekocht in een speciale chocolade winkel in Gent, dat deed ze toen ze al zwaar zwanger liep terwijl de Scheldestroom daar 200ton zand was aan het lossen bij de glasfabriek. Hij zou over een paar uur weer naar Gent toe zeilen zodra de felicitaties voorbij waren. Kees stond bekend voor zijn humanitaire hulp tijdens de Eerste Wereldoorlog toen Nederland neutraal was en België werd binnengevallen. Hij voer met zijn varende rivierklipper De Scheldestroom, beladen met voedsel en medicijnen om de armoede van de door oorlog geteisterde Belgische bevolking te verlichten. Iedereen wist dat de Duitsers en de Engelsen op zijn schip schoten. Toch zeilde De Scheldestroom er doorheen. Ze noemden het het wonderschip en de vrome katholieke Belg zag de hand van God over dit goede schip.

De dames van het stadhuis wilden weten hoe Kees en Francine met een extra kind zouden omgaan, omdat de woonruimte op De Scheldestroom beperkt was. Het had slechts één kleine roef die dienst deed als woon- en slaapverblijf plus keuken, wc- washok voor twee volwassenen en nu, met de geboorte van Piet, vier kinderen. Kees vertelde hen dat ze erin geslaagd waren om elke kleine ruimte te benutten. Piets babybedje was de romp van een nog niet afgemaakt Tjalk-modelschip dat Kees aan het bouwen was voor koningin Wilhelmina. Het was voorbestemd dat Piets hele jeugd op De Scheldestroom zou worden doorgebracht. Dezelfde loop herhaalde zich twee jaar later weer op een zeer koude en winderige vroege donderdagochtend 17 november 1926. Zijn houten schippersschoenen kletterden en echoden alweer over de geplaveide stenen op naar het Stadhuis in Terneuzen om de geboorte van zijn derde zoon Cornelis Paulusse te melden. De nieuwe baby werd Kees genoemd bijna alle jongens in Nederland die Cornelis waren werden meestal Kees genoemd, wel een oer Nederlandse naam. Opnieuw gaf Kees alle 7 ambtenaren op het stadhuis een grote dure sigaar. Francine had in Antwerpen drie doosjes vol met verschillende soorten verse romige Belgische chocolaatjes gekocht en deze werden gegeven aan de vrouwelijke ambtenaren die daar ook bezig waren. Er was een reden voor zijn vrijgevigheid, diezelfde ambtenaren gaven ook verscheidene vergunningen uit voor dit en het andere, evenals het innen van gemeentelijke belastingen voor maritieme diensten aan de scheepvaart; het loonde om aan hun goede kant te staan, nee het was geen omkoping maar het pienter opbouwen van subtiele relaties en netwerken. En wederom op donderdag 28 juni 1928 begaf Kees zich naar het stadhuis van Terneuzen om de geboorte van Abraham Paulusse, zijn vierde zoon, innemend Bram genoemd weer te melden. Opnieuw werden de sigaren aangestoken en de Belgische chocolade bonbons uitgedeeld. Dit keer had Kees haast. De Scheldestroom moest binnen een uur de haven verlaten, beladen met tonnen aardappelen, uien en erwten met als bestemming Amsterdam. Er was extra voedsel nodig voor de duizenden atleten en bezoekers van de IXOlympic Games in Amsterdam die op 28 juli 1928 begonnen. Ook vertelde hij, niet zonder veel trots, dat enkele jaren geleden de Scheldestroom met andere varende klippers de miljoenen lokaal gebakken stenen leverde voor de bouw van het Art Deco Olympisch Stadion en de Olympische vlam toren. De Olympische vlam maakte daar zijn eerste verschijning in de moderne tijd en werd aangestoken bovenop de bakstenen toren die uitkijkt over het Olympisch Stadion.

Opvallend hierbij is dat tijdens de oorlogsperiode 1914-1918 geen Paulusse kinderen werden geboren. Francine zei dat dit een opzettelijke daad van gezinsplanning was, ze vond het niet verstandig om kinderen te baren als Engeland, Duitsland of Frankrijk Nederland elk moment zou kunnen binnenvallen. Ze had de erbarmelijke toestand gezien van vluchtelingen met hun huilende baby's, kleuters en jonge kinderen. Ze hadden besloten geen baby's meer zo lang neutraal Nederland voortdurend werd bedreigd met inslag van oorlog dat elk moment kon gebeuren. Kees zei ook dat het eigenlijk helemaal niet veilig was om met de Scheldestroom te zeilen, "je zou maar op een drijvende mijn varen en dan was het gedaan." Trouwens het schip kon ook zo in beslag kunnen worden genomen door oorlog voerende landen zoals Duitsland, Engeland en Frankrijk", zei hij. Ze hadden deskundig advies gelezen over "stoppen" en de andere over de "spreiding" van geboorten van ene dr. Rutgers, een opkomende Nederlandse deskundige op het gebied van gezinsplanning.  Toen Bram werd geboren was hun oudste dochter Bette al 17 jaar oud en werkte ze als huishoudster bij een rijke weduwnaar, *een rijke stinkerd* zei Francine in Gent. Hun oudste zoon Jan -Pieter was 16 en was leerling-monteur en woonde aan de wal in het huis van zijn toekomstige echtgenote Bets van der Hooft. Dochter Jana het op één na oudste meisje was net 15 geworden en zorgde voor haar bejaarde grootouders opa en oma van Aalst die in de Java buurt woonden. Deze gezinsgroei was gespreid omdat het roefje aan de Scheldestroom niet alle zes kinderen en twee ouders tegelijk konden bergen. Zodra Piet vijf jaar oud was verhuisde hij naar 'het vooronder', een kleine ruimte aan de boeg van het schip waar reserve zeilen en touwen werden gestouwd. Kees had de stalen platen bekleed met houtfineer en isolatie materiaal. Er was ruimte voor drie bedden en later gebruikten de drie jongens het als hun slaapkamer. Ik had me vaak afgevraagd over persoonlijke hygiëne in zulke kleine ruimtes. Op een dag vroeg ik Francine er naar, ze zei dat iedereen die aan boord woonde elke dag hun hele lichaam en haar moesten wassen met 'groene zeep' vertelde ze erbij. Nee zei ze, "dat is niet de Nederlandse gewoonte om je elke dag te wassen, de gemiddelde Nederlander gaat maar één keer per week zichzelf helemaal wassen en dan nog maar niet te spreken om een stel ondergoed voor een hele week te dragen. *Vuulakken zijn het.* Francine wist dat wij in Australië minstens één keer per dag een douche of bad namen en schoon ondergoed verfrissen, nee dat vond ze wel proper.

In de kleine roef was er een soort 'was- kast' ter grootte van een klein douche-celletje met een diep waterbassin gevuld door een elektrische waterpomp. In de winter werd het water warm gehouden met een elektronisch element dat Kees in de kleine verswatertank had gemonteerd. In de zomermaanden sprongen de mannen gewoon over boord in het kristalheldere water, toen waren de meeste kanalen in die tijd niet zo vervuild als heden met chemicaliën, oliën en plastic. Men kon nog steeds schuimen met zeep, omdat het water er niet hard was en geen hoge concentratie calcium- en magnesiumionen had. Het was nodig om zich elke dag te wassen omdat soms de lading in de Scheldestroom vuil en stoffig was, zoals modderstof van aardappelen en suikerbieten of steenkoolvuil dat eruit sijpelde door hessionzakken, gevuld met kolen. Niemand van de familie zou ongewassen en met werkkleding de roef binnenkomen. Francine was altijd trots dat ze de eerste elektrische wasmachine in Zeeuws-Vlaanderen liet maken, door Kees natuurlijk, die had een elektromotor op haar hand gedraaide waskuip geïnstalleerd. Mensen kwamen van heinde en verre kijken. Eigenlijk was het geen nieuw idee want Kees had al een elektrische wasmachine gezien bij de wereldtentoonstelling van Parijs in 1900.

Francine en Kees gaven al hun kinderen homeschoolonderwijs met behulp van een homeschool-syllabus die was ontworpen voor schipperskinderen, bestaande uit oefenboeken die de nadruk legden op de belangrijke drie, lezen schrijven en rekenen. Deze syllabussen waren in overeenstemming met elke school in het land. Als ze op vracht zaten te wachten gingen de kinderen naar de plaatselijke school en na de basisschool studeerden de jongens aan technische hogescholen en logeerden ze bij Bette of Janna of bij tantes of ooms, die toen aan wal woonden of werkten.

*"Optimistische vastberaden originaliteit en creativiteit"* hadden het motto van de familie Paulusse moeten zijn. Dit wil niet zeggen dat er nooit lastige problemen zijn geweest, want elk gezin heeft gewoonlijk een of ander kwaad te verdragen. De oudere broer van Kees was Abraham gewoon Bram genoemd. Oom Bram had ook een zeilklipper die een paar tonnen zwaarder was dan de Scheldestroom en twee masten had, het heette "Elizabeth" naar hun moeder. De Scheldestroom en de Elizabeth waren als het ware een item van de broers Paulusse. Opa Kees en oom Bram, beidde altijd een oogje in het zeil voor elkander, zorgden voor elkaars zakelijke gezondheid en welzijn. Ze deelden vaak vracht en werkten samen en vaak als één eenheid. Bram is nooit getrouwd geweest, zijn moeder liet hem beloven voor zijn jongere broer Jan te zorgen die een geestelijke handicap had. Als jong kind speelde deze oom Jan met mij op een vriendelijke manier, maar toch wel plagend op pestend na. Als ik hem op straat tegenkwam kauwend op tabak bood hij vol enthousiasme een ' tabakspruim' aan wat ik als kleine jongen erg vies vond maar hij vond het schitterend, een misplaatste, jeugdige humor vind ik nu. Ik ben er bijna zeker van dat hij op het spectrum van autistisch iets had en aan bipolair leed. Niet dat hij zo werd gediagnosticeerd. Als psychologiestudent las ik dingen waarin ik oom Jan erkende. Als zesjarige herinner ik me zijn bijna ongecontroleerde driftbuien. Ik was echter verrast dat hij nog nooit overboord was gevallen en verdronken, hij kon niet zwemmen. Jan vaarde 30 jaar lang als matroos op de Elizabeth, maar ze moesten voor het meest van deze tijd een oppas voor hem inhuren. Kees en Francine, en trouwens de hele Paulusse familie, ontfermden zich over oom Jan. Dat moest wel want er was toen geen verzorgingsstaat zoals nu is en er waren ook geen medicijnen die konden helpen zoals nu.

Ze noemden het de roerige jaren twintig, langzamerhand kende Nederland een economische groei die negen jaar duurden. De huis comforts zoals wasmachines, koelkasten, stofzuigers en radio's werden allemaal gemaakt door Phillips Electronics in Nederland. Andere producten zoals de *Spijker-auto's* waren populair bij de duizenden 'nouveau riche' die hun fortuin hadden verdiend in de zwarte handel tijdens de Eerste Wereldoorlog. De groeiende economie zorgde voor een optimistisch gevoel over de toekomst. Kees was zich er terdege van bewust dat de nieuwe economische situatie veel kansen voor welvaart bood. Ook erkende hij dat veel gebieden in Nederland niet deelden in de economische welvaart. De omstandigheden van de Paulusse en hun Scheldestroom waren goed, er was geen schuld. Schippers met te kleine boten hadden het moeilijk om te concurreren op de wilde vaart om vracht. De Scheldestroom had het geluk dat er veel werk was voor dit type zeilschip omdat motorbrandstof en kolen nog gerantsoeneerd waren en Kees concurreerde op prijs en snelheid. Van zijn vriend Loe Boone, een Terneuzens garagehouder op de Axelsestraat kreeg hij een oude Ford model T-motor die Kees zelf volledig reviseerde en in de roeiboot van de Scheldestroom vestigde. Zo werd de roeiboot een soort duw- trek- minisleepboot. Het bespaarde veel geld dat ze anders zouden moeten betalen voor sleepboten die nodig waren om ze door de vele kanaalsluizen te trekken. Francine en de meisjes hoefden de Scheldestroom niet meer lopend en met de hand te trekken. Ze leverden ook minisleepdiensten aan, aan andere zeilklippers.

De Scheldestroom was altijd in de Wilde Vaart geweest, wat betekent dat er allerlei soorten ongeregelde vrachtvervoer was. Het was competitief en winstgevender omdat er geen tussenpersoon nodig was die veel geld spaarde, het enige nadeel was dat men moest socialiseren en onderhandelen over een Hollandse jenever of bier met klanten in de aangewezen vrachtcafés. Af en toe kwam Kees licht dronken thuis en Francine vond het niet prettig omdat ze bang was dat hij van de loopplank zou vallen en zou verdrinken, iets wat jammer genoeg heel veel gebeurde. Kees, met zijn broer Bram, onderhielden waardevolle netwerken en zaken en relaties met vrienden; bekenden in de wereld van de scheepvaart en vrachtafhandeling. Vandaag zou ik zeggen dat ze een onschatbaar *sociaal kapitaal* hadden. Een scheepvaartfamilie als de gastvrije Paulusse, maakten onvermijdelijk vrienden in elke haven. Er kwamen altijd stromen van interessante bezoekers, vrienden en vijanden aan boord van de Scheldestroom voor koffie en gezelligheid.

De 1920 jaren waren een bonanza voor de Paulusse en in alle opzichten werden gezonde kinderen geboren. Welvaart en nieuwe technologie was koning, maar de goede tijd stortte in, in 1929. Beginnend met de crash van de New York Stock Exchange, de gevolgen herleefden over de hele wereld, inclusief Nederland. Wat moest er worden gedaan ...één ding dat volstrekt niet gedaan moest worden, en dat was bij de pakken neer te zitten.

# HOOFSTUK 5

*Van crises tot overvloed voort op eigen kracht,*
*maar zoals gezegd waren ze 'survivors' van nature*
*en niet snel afgeschrikt door de tegenstand.*

De moeilijkheden voor Kees en Francine begonnen in 1931 toen er geen vracht meer vervoerd werd. Er waren geen vrachten meer. De Fabrieken waren gesloten, de economische depressie was ingetreden. De laatste paar vrachten van de Scheldestroom waren het dumpen van 400 ton aardappelen in de Noordzee in opdracht van de Nederlandse regering, *de vissen waren er blij mee,* zo schreef Kees eens op een ansichtkaart gestuurd vanuit Scheveningen.

Ze walgden absoluut van de grove onbekwaamheid van de Nederlandse premier Hendrik Colijn en zijn conservatieve rechtse partij, terwijl honderdduizenden Nederlanders met honger naar bed gingen en niet in staat waren om hun gezin naar behoren te voeden van de extreem magere overheidsondersteuning dat ze kregen. De regering gaf opdracht om al het plantaardig voedsel te vernietigen dat niet verkocht kon worden omdat de mensen geen werk hadden en consequent geen geld voor levensonderhoud en inkopen te doen, laat staan voedsel.

Dit alles schiep een klimaat van somber pessimisme, moedeloosheid en bitterheid onder de honderdduizenden werkloze Nederlanders. Het was een tijd van grote beproeving, ook voor Francine en Kees en hun schip Scheldestroom. *wat moet er allemaal van kommen* vroegen ze zich af.

*Nee de Belgen doen het beter* vertelde Francine over haar verre neef, de briljante *Paul van Zeeland*, die toen premier van België was. Hij had een veel betere aanpak om deze vreselijke economische crises te beheersen. Hij garandeerde 4% rente op spaargeld en bevroor alle prijzen en verbood de vernietiging van broodnodig voedsel. Daarna sloeg ze Hendrik Colijn af en zijn onbekwame handlangers om. De Paulusses deden zoveel ze konden en smokkelden aardappelen naar een geheim pakhuis. Hun kinderen Jan-Pieter, Bette en Janna vulden grote jutezakken vol met aardappelen in totaal 400 kilo en staken deze weg op de Scheldestroom en op zusterschip *de Elizabeth*.

Kees fabriceerde een aardappelen-raspmachine, vervaardigt om aardappelmeel tot gedroogd poeder te maken, dat nam niet zoveel ruimte in als zakken aardappelen.

Alle zusters van Aalst kwamen aan boord en hielpen met het bottelen van groenten en fruit zoals bonen, erwten, rode bieten en wortelen, groenten die als het waren gered of beter gezegd gestolen waren van vernietiging. *In deze zaak gedeerd gestolen goed wel* zei de familie in latere gesprekken. *Ja inderdaad'* zei Kees, '*wij hebben nogal wat voedsel achterover gedrukt om aan de arme stakkers te geven in het noorden van het land waar te kort was en honger heerste.* Niet te geloven he van de regering die dan zogenaamd een coalitie is van Christelijke partijen, en dan al de groenten zomaar dumpen of kalkpoeder er over strooiden, daar deugt niks van en het heeft geen ziel geholpen enkel maar narigheid. *Jezus zal wel gehuild hebben'* zei Kees dan met een knipoog. Een deel van dit voedsel was voor eigen gebruik, maar het meeste werd door de zusters van Aalst omgeleid en uitgedeeld aan de werklozen van Terneuzen.

Verschillende Belgische zaken lui die vluchtelingen waren Kees' hulpvaardigheid bij het uitbreken van de Eerste Wereldoorlog voor de Belgen niet vergeten en gaven hem gedurende enige tijd in de depressie nog vrachten voor de Scheldestroom en de Elizabeth om naar het westen van Nederland aardappelen en suikerbieten te vervoeren. Goed Karma krijgt goede daden.

De tijd was gekomen dat er geen vrachtwerk meer was, alles was gestopt en duizenden schippers waren geruïneerd, vooral die op de Rijn van en naar Duitsland voeren. De Scheldestroom werd door Kees zelf vrijwillig gemeerd en het gebruik van het schip werd omgetoverd naar een soort drijvend scheepsbouwonderhoudscentrum. Op dat moment was zijn eerste zoon Jan-Pieter Paulusse een autoreparatiebedrijf begonnen in Terneuzen, mogelijk gemaakt met financiële hulp van zijn ouders Kees en Francien. Jan-Pieter zijn garage had het erg druk vanwege zijn goede reputatie van vakmanschap en vriendelijkheid en zijn woord was goud. Wat hij beloofde kwam hij na.

De zaken zoals oude motoren reviseren voor nieuwe en zijn vader Kees kocht deze motoren weer voor zijn cliënten. *Ze zeggen dat noodzaak de moeder van de uitvinding is. Dit was zeker waar in het geval van de Paulusses.* De vrachtruimen van de Scheldestroom werden al snel omgebouwd tot een behoorlijke werkplaats. Zoals reparatie, verf en constructie waar Kees gewone roeiboten zou ombouwen tot push-pull boten door zijn gereviseerde motoren in deze boten te plaatsen. Andere kleine werkboten werden omgebouwd tot luxe zeilboten. Een krant in Terneuzen rapporteerde dat:

> *'Toen de economische depressie ook de binnenvaart voor een groot gedeelte van het jaar lamlegde en de "Scheldestroom "aangemeerd lag in het midden kanaalarm aan de trambrug, ging Paulusse motors plaatsen in sloepen en jachten en onderving hiermede het gedwongen niets doen. Eigenlijk is dit niet helemaal juist, want niets doen ligt niet in de aard van de heer Paulusse. Toen in 1908 de eerste binnenmotoren de zogenaamde "Renes- Motor",die werd gestookt met blanke olie op heel bescheiden schaal, de zeilen ging vervangen had Paulusse voor deze nieuwe vorm van vaartechniek een levende interesse. Omstreeks 1920 zette de kentering zich nog verder voort en verscheen de ruwe olie motor. Omstreeks de dertiger jaren bracht Paulusse een motor de z.g. opduwer, aan zijn roeiboot. Toen was al*

*gebleken dat hij feeling had voor scheepsmotoren. In zijn
weinige vrije uren repareerde hij zo nu en dan motoren van
de schippers en ook wel van auto's en steeds meer kwamen
zijn collega's aan boord om zijn raad in te winnen.*

*-Ter Neuzensche Courant November 1932*

Hij kreeg een grote opdracht van de welvarende familie Vermast uit
Terneuzen om hun grote roeiboot om te bouwen tot een zeilend jacht.
Alleen deze klus nam al zes maanden in beslag. Kees nam ook andere
mannen in dienst in zijn nieuwe onderneming. Ik heb een foto van *"De
zwerver"* geplaatst, zo noemden ze het voltooide jacht.

De Zwerver van Vermast is nu klaar en word uit het ruim van de
Scheldestroom gehesen. Janna met haar vader Kees houden het in
balance. Er was heel veel belangstelling.

Dochters Jana en Bette en hun jonge broers leerden ook hoe ze moesten
schilderen en roest van de ijzeren dekken bikken. Alle banen waren voor
alle geslachten. 'Meisjes konden net zo goed werk leveren als jongens'
zei hij. 'Soms zelfs beter. Zijn reputatie als ambachtsman was algemeen

bekend, aangezien zijn hobby het maken van vintage scheepsmodellen was. Deze modellen werden verkocht aan musea, koningen en koninginnen. Terwijl ik onderzoek deed voor dit boek vond ik een krantenartikel uit 1960 in de krant "Het Vrij Volk".

Hier is de vertaling van het artikel:

> *"De oude schipper Paulusse uit Terneuzen kan het scheepsleven niet vergeten. Zijn liefde voor de zee en zijn knutseltalenten kwamen bijzonder goed tot uitdrukking toen hij vele jaren geleden een wiegje voor zijn zoon maakte. Het bruine houten baby-bed nam vanzelf de vorm van een rank en slank schip aan. Later, verteld de heer Paulusse; "Toen mijn zoon uit de wieg was gegroeid heb ik een dek in het geval gemaakt en het verder opgetuigd.'t is een pracht van een model geworden, waar we ook werkelijk mee op zee konden zeilen."*
>
> *De 80 jarige schipper eens in de "wilde vaart", vindt zijn dagelijkse bezigheden nog steeds te midden van vele zeilschepen, miniatuurzeilboten wel te verstaan. Wanneer hij alle scheepjes die hij in de loop der jaren bouwde nog bij elkaar had zou waarschijnlijk zijn grote huiskamer nog te klein zijn om de hele voorraad te bergen. "Ik ben al vanaf m'n zestiende jaar met deze hobby bezig. Kun je nagaan dat ik er heel wat gemaakt moet hebben." Er bestaat bijzonder veel belangstelling voor de miniatuur zeilschepen van de Terneuzense oud schipper. Hij heeft zijn vaste afnemers, verspreid over heel Nederland. Deze klanten betaalden graag zo'n vier- tot vijfhonderd gulden per exemplaar. De maker heeft er dan ook een maand of zes weken iedere dag een tiental uren aan gewerkt in het nauwe bijkeukentje dat hij als atelier heeft ingericht. Schipper Paulusse's collectie moet wel heel wat pronkstukken omvatten. Hij bouwde "de Groene Draeck" van Prinses Beatrix en maakte een*

*schip dat als huwelijksgeschenk voor Koningin Fabiola en
Koning Boudewijn van België moest dienen enzovoorts.*

*Helaas hebben we ze niet kunnen bewonderen.*

*"Zodra ik er eentje af heb klopt er weer een afnemer aan de
deur. t'Lijkt wel of ze het ruiken, mijn producten vliegen
gewoon weg. Enfin, dat kun je wel zien voor jezelf ik heb
er nooit één over kunnen houden."*

Ik herinner me de familiegesprekken die we hadden over de Grote
Depressie zoals we die in Australië noemen. De honderdduizenden
werkloze Nederlanders leidden halverwege de jaren dertig een somber
en vaak uitzichtloos bestaan. De beelden uit de jaren dertig zijn dan
ook vaak van een somber decennium. Maar de werklozen waren slechts
een - helaas veel te grote - minderheid. Aan de andere kant was er
echter een meerderheid die wel een baan had, en die meerderheid was
niet persé slechter af dan voorheen vanwege de dalende prijzen. Er was
geen overheidsuitreiking voor schippers zoals Kees en Bram, maar zoals
gezegd waren ze 'survivors' van nature en niet snel afgeschrikt door de
tegenstand. Ondanks dit alles om meer vrolijke muziek in hun leven
te brengen, kochten ze een Phillips Punt Radio. Het was een art deco-
ontwerp gemaakt van prachtig hout. Ik heb het nog steeds in mijn bezit
en het heeft een geheel eigen verhaal voor later in dit boek, en ja het
werkt nog steeds! Tijdens deze crisis jaren werden veel liedjes geschreven
om de stemmingen en de goede geesten op te heffen, versjes zoals '
Happy days are here again', maar Kees's favoriete liedje, wat hij mij
ook leerde zingen als jong kind, was een versje met een zeer opzwepend
aanstekelijk deuntje van ene Bob Scholten:

*"Breng eens een zonnetje onder de mensen
Een blij gezicht te zien
Dat doet toch goed
Vervul zo nu en dan Hun liefste wensen
Het spreekwoord zegt Wie goed doet goed ontmoet*

*Het leven is geen pretje*
*Ben je bedrukt, verzet je*
*Als je 't geluk wilt zoeken*
*'t Hangt aan een zijden draad*
*Als je succes wilt boeken*
*Luister naar mijne raad"*

Voor de zoveelste keer in haar kaarten en brieven raadde oma Francine mij aan dat ik altijd naar de positieve kant moest kijken:

*'Wat jouw aandacht ook trekt, krijg jij.'*

Ze benadrukte de succesverhalen uit de jaren dertig zoals de triomf van de KLM Uiver die deelnam aan de legendarische race van Londen naar Melbourne in oktober 1934, waarin 21 vliegtuigen strijden om zo snel mogelijk de halve wereld rond te vliegen.

De KLM-bemanning was succesvol: de Uiver landde na ruim negentig uur als tweede in Melbourne en behaalde de eerste plaats in de handicap na het maken van een noodlanding op Albury en was door de burgers van Albury uit de modder getrokken.

Kees zei dat de prestatie van de Uiver een symbool was van de modernisering van Nederland en stimuleerde het om een wereldleider in de luchtvaart te zijn door de vliegtuigfabrieken van KLM en Anthony Fokkers. O, en vergeet uiteindelijk niet de doorbraak van de fiets als populair vervoermiddel. Van de jaren dertig waren er ongeveer 3,5 miljoen fietsen op een bevolking van 8 miljoen mensen.

In 1959, terwijl tante Leine en oma Francine aan het bottelen waren in hun kleine keuken in de Dahliastraat 7, vroeg ik hun over dingen waar ze zich zorgen over hadden gemaakt tijdens de crisisjaren. Hebben ze zich ooit zorgen gemaakt? Ze barstten in lachen uit, zeker! Maar het was meer een gezonde en beheerste stress dan een zeurend, zorgwekkend gevoel.

Ze dachten dat stress niet erg was, het hielp hen 's ochtends op te staan. 'Ik veronderstel', zei oma, 'dat ik eerder bezorgd dan gestrest was zoals het welzijn van mijn kinderen en Kees die allemaal samen in een drijvend bad woonden dat ieder moment kon zinken', knipoogde ze.

*'Varen op de Scheldestroom in ruige zeeën, golven donderend op de krakende dek-luiken, alles schuddend en zien hoe arme Kees worstelde met het voeren van de zeilen. Zijn kleren kletsnat, ik aan het roerwiel en de kinderen alleen in de Roef. Ze speelden, alsof er niets aan de hand was, met puzzels of een bordspel.*

Er was geen tijd voor stress, angst of zorgen, want we kenden de zee. En het schip verkeerde in goede staat. De kinderen waren er aan gewend ookal ging de Scheldestroom soms flink tekeer, het was allemaal normaal. Gewoon een deel van het schippers beroep.

De kinderen begrepen dat, maar hun veiligheid stond altijd op de eerste plaats en van baby af aan konden ze allemaal zwemmen.'

'Ja', ging Francine verder, "Een Economische crisis was net zoals slecht weer. Maar uiteindelijk kwamen we er wel overheen, kijk hoe Kees en mijn jongens en de meiden het goed deden tijdens alle tegenspoed. O, ze hadden zo'n veerkracht.

'Ik ben een trotse moeder hoor, zonder schaamte'!' zei ze dan.

Tante Leine bevestigde,' ja hetzelfde met mijn kinderen. Ze overleefden en bloeiden ondanks dat ons schip werd gebombardeerd door de moffen. Maar ik moet iets verklappen over dat zwemmen van haar kinderen. Weet je dat je oma nooit heeft kunnen zwemmen? Maar er was altijd een levensreddende boei bij de hand voor oma, in geval als ze eens in het water mocht vallen.' zei Leine lachend. 'Maar goed, ze heeft veertig jaar op de Scheldestroom gewoond en is nooit in het water gevallen.'

Opa Kees die in de buurt van het keukentje aan één van zijn modellen had gewerkt en stilletjes meeluisterde, was het ermee eens dat zoveel van zijn tijdgenoten zich letterlijk dood hadden gekweld zonder actie te ondernemen.Tegenslag is iets dat we kunnen overwinnen, terwijl een psychische stoornis iets is dat we moeten beheersen zoals we deden met mijn broer Jan en zijn mentale problemen. *Maak je geen zorgen! Wees gelukkig!"*, zei hij jaren voordat het nummer populair werd gemaakt.

Tijdens deze periode van economische crisis en later tijdens de Tweede Wereldoorlog waren er zelden voedseltekorten op de Scheldestroom. Francine had een gouden koord aan haar boog, ze was een fantastische kok en daarom noemde ik haar "Oma Chef" niets was pakketvoedsel of gefabriceerd voedsel. Op dat moment waren er geen koelkasten aan boord, al het vlees werd gerookt of in grote stenen potten gedaan.

De gefrituurde schnitzels en het spek worden allemaal in zijn eigen vet bewaard en kunnen maanden worden bewaard in grote zware stenen potten. In die tijd hadden ze geen koelkast aan boord. Ze zou zuurkool maken van kool en zout dat wekenlang gewekt onder zout lag te verzuren tot het klaar was, waarna grote porties werden uitgedeeld aan de vrienden en familie van de buren.

Het bottelen van groenten en fruit op tijd van overvloed was een activiteit waar alle zusters van Aalst aan deelnamen. Omdat het veel werk was om groenten te reinigen en te 'blancheren' voorafgaand aan het bottelen, (reinigt het oppervlak van vuil en organismen) verheldert de kleur en helpt het verlies van vitamines vertragen. Francine bakte al haar eigen soorten brood in de kleine oven die Kees zelf had gemaakt. Ook tijdens de Tweede Wereldoorlog werd er voedsel uit hun lading geknepen, vooral voedsel dat bestemd was voor Duitsland.

Kees vervaardigde een speciale metalen pijp die eruitzag als een grote holle naald die voorzichtig door de treden van de jutezakken werd geperst waarna de suiker door de metalen voorraadpijp in een container stroomde. Hetzelfde gebeurde voor granen, melasse en erwten. Ik vroeg tante Leine en haar zus Francine over zorgen, 'ja we maakten ons veel zorgen' zeiden ze, 'maar zorgen zijn natuurlijk, het is een goede zaak, want het zorgt ervoor dat je nadenkt over wat je moet doen. Als je geen actie onderneemt, dan word je depressief.'

Ik was het er mee eens dat zoveel van zijn tijdgenoten zich zoveel zorgen maakten zonder actie te ondernemen. 'Tegenslag is iets dat we kunnen overwinnen, terwijl een psychische stoornis iets is dat moet worden beheerd zoals we doen met oom Jan en zijn mentale problemen. De labels impliceren heel andere mogelijkheden. Maak je geen zorgen, wees blij.' zei ze, een jaar voordat het lied populair werd.

## *Gezellig in de Roef bijeen.*

De familie kwam dikwijls bijeen in de roef van de Scheldestroom waar hartelijke inhoudende gesprekken onder het spelen van spelletjes plaats vonden ten midden van zoete tabak dat Kees rookte. Iedereen vond de zoete reuk van de rook lekker en meestal als aangenaam ervaren en zeer gezellig. *Dan nog met de koffiegeur en muziek van de nieuwe 78 toeren platenspeler die ze geruild hadden. "voor een grote zak aardappelen ergens in Olland', zei Francine. 'Want die arme stakkers kwamen bijna om van de grote vrete '.* Natuurlijk waren er goede ontwikkelde gesprekken in deze crisistijd zoals de waaroms en hoezo's en wie het laatste antwoord had.

De vele familiebrieven gaven dat het niet slecht was voor iedereen. De depressiejaren waren geen slechte jaren voor gezinnen die voor overlevingsinstincten hadden getraind en degenen die buiten het speelplein creatief konden denken, die iets anders durfden te proberen en niet bedaard waren om nieuwe kansen te grijpen en te ontwikkelen.

'Ja', voegde Leine er aan toe. 'Mensen die het meeste van hun tijd een zonnig karakter hebben zijn in staat om veel problemen op te lossen. De nevel en mist in hun hersenen wordt, bij wijze van spreken, weggejaagd door de zon en er komt duidelijkheid en een doel naar voren.'

Ze vond het jammer dat hier in Nederland er zoveel mensen zijn zoals Minister President Hendrick Colijn, die geloven in de calvinistische leer dat zegt dat het karakter van de mensheid totaal volslagen verdorvenheid en onwaardig is. 't's toch wat', Leine ging door, ' om zo te denken over jezelf en je naaste mens. Van geen wonder dat er zoveel pessimisme is onder het volk. Bah! Vlug Kees, draai dat plaatje van Bob Scholten nog eens… van een zonnetje te zijn.'

'ben eens een zonnetje onder de mensen een blij gezicht te zien doet je toch goed'… Iedereen in de Roef zong mee. Gezellig, zo hartelijk en menselijk. Absoluut geen volslagen verdorvenheid.

Francine en Kees bepaalden de waarde van spaarzaamheid, recycling, maken en vervaardigen van dingen, maar waren wel zeer vrijgevig jegens hun medemens.

Hun eigen voorbeeld en praktijk van verdraagzaamheid in zeer moeilijke economische tijden versterkten hun zelfredzaamheid en leerden hun kinderen overlevingsvaardigheden. Vooral over hoe ze tijdens deze crisisjaren konden gedijen. In één van zijn brieven aan mij schreef opa Kees dat deze vaardigheden op het gebied van overleven niet op school of universiteit worden onderwezen. En met gevoel voor humor zei hij dat ze daar de jongens niet leren om hun eigen wol te spinnen en sokken te breien. 'Nou, mijn jongens kunnen dat wel. Zij hebben geen wol- en breifabrieken nodig.' De textiel- en wolfabrieken waren bijna allemaal door de crises gesloten in Nederland, waardoor zo'n 20.000 textielarbeiders zonder werk en zo maar op straat werden gegooid. Er waren weinig mensen of instanties die zich ontfermden over deze mensen., De kerken' zei Kees, 'trokken aan hetzelfde lijntje van Colijn.'

Een bevooroordeelde houding, niet gebaseerd op enig onderzoek. Hendrik Colijn dacht dat als de staat te veel hulp zouden bieden aan werklozen, dan zouden deze lui worden en niet vlug willen werken en zouden ze besmet worden met de luie ziekte. In 1932 opende Francine spaarrekeningen voor elk haar kinderen. Daar zag ik bewijs van in mijn schoenendoos vol met bewaarde herinneringen met ook de verlopen spaarbankboekjes van de Paulusse-kinderen. Ze lagen voor mij met nog de kinder-vingerafdrukken op de kaften van de spaarbankboekjes.

Elke maand liepen de twee ventjes Piet en Kees naar het loket van de Rijks Post Bank om persoonlijk hun guldens op hun spaarrekening te zetten die ze zelf verdient hadden. En met een glimlach die een zekere mate van trots aangaf over hun prestaties en vermogen om geld te verdienen. En terecht, het is geen kleinigheid om toen vier tot vijf, soms tien gulden per maand op de bank te storten. Deze bedragen verdienden Piet en Kees als tieners die met hun oudere zus Janna oude kranten verzamelden en die,doordrenkt met water, met de hand dan geperst en gerold werden als een bal en om vervolgens te laten drogen in de zon of bij de kachel in de roef.

Er was veel vraag voor hun producten en mensen kwamen deze papierenballen ophalen daar waar ook de Scheldestroom gemeerd lag. De papieren brandballen waren goedkoper dan steenkool en duurzamer. Of het waar is weet ik niet maar dat was hun marketing- en verkoopmotto. Waar geen geld was, zouden ze goederen en diensten ruilen.


## Trouwerijen.

Naast de economische depressie, die zoveel energie en levenslust opslokte voor de honderdduizenden Nederlanders om te overleven was er ook aandacht voor andere gesprekken op de Scheldestroom. De gesprekken veranderden in trouwen en getrouwd zijn en de voorbereiding voor de feesten van slechts drie huwelijken die binnenkort gevierd zouden worden. De naaimachines en de breinaalden aan boord van de Scheldestroom werden vooral rond de jaren 1938 en 1939 bezig gehouden met het maken van jurken, broeken, shirts en stropdassen. De jongens die hun eigen wollen sokken breiden en Francine die een heel grote oranje wimpel naait, om samen met het rood-wit-blauw van de vlag bovenop de hoge mast van de Scheldestroom te hijzen om het huwelijk van kroonprinses Juliana met de Duitse prins Bernhard te vieren op een zeer koude donderdag 7 januari 1937.

Hun eerstgeboren zoon, Jan-Pieter, trouwde op donderdag 13 oktober 1938 met Elizabeth van der Hooft.

Janna, hun tweede dochter, trouwde na zes jaar verloofd te zijn geweest met haar oude geliefde Adriaan de Zeeuw in 1939.

Kees en Francine betaalden voor beide huwelijksrecepties bij Cafe De Vriendschap.

Ze hadden het goed gedaan tijdens de depressie. Niet dankzij de overheid, nee ze voeren met hun eigen schip door zeer stormachtige zeeën en bereikten veilig de kalme wateren. In mei 1939 kwam er een telegram. Jan Pieter moest zich dringend melden bij de Vlissingen marinebasis.

# HOOFTSTUK 6

itler had Polen in 1939 aangevallen en Kees' 'intuïtieve gevoelens voorspelden dat het niet lang zou duren voordat nazi-Duitsland Nederland zou binnenvallen. Ik dacht altijd dat intuïtief zijn een geschenk van de goden was, omdat er moed voor nodig is om intuïtie te volgen. Net als voor de Eerste Wereldoorlog werden ook dit keer alle mannen boven de 18 gemobiliseerd, waardoor de Scheldestroom zijn matroos verloor aan het leger. Toen mijn vader Piet nog maar 15 jaar oud was werkte hij op een Belgische binnenvaart-olietanker genaamd 'Nijverheid', geschipperd door zijn oom Gerit Tanis die getrouwd was met Marie, de jongste van de van Aalst zussen. Ook zíj woonden op hun schip zowel als hun neef matroos Piet.

De Nijverheid werd door de Belgische overheid aangewezen als vitale olietransporter die door de dreigende oorlogsomstandigheden defensiepersoneel aan boord plaatste. Zodoende ging Piet weer aan het werk bij zijn vader op de Scheldestroom. Tot op zekere hoogte waren dit idyllische tijden, de stilte voor de storm, er was een onheilspellend gevoel onder de bevolking. De Schelde van ouds is verbluffend. Het stromende zoete water nog onvervuild met veel vis, vooral paling die klaar is om te vangen. Vaak zag men sierlijke varende rivierklippers, verleidelijk om de volle bruin gekleurde zeilen te aanschouwen met hun zwaar eikenhouten zwaarden. De schippers die prachtig navigeerden in alle weersomstandigheden die met loeven tegen de wind op zeilen, en om te zien hoe de voorstevens van de fraaie klippers naar de wind draaien.

Piet was inmiddels de eerste matroos op de Scheldestroom van zijn vader en hield zich bezig met onderhoudsschuren, het schilderen van de luiken en het nooit afgelopen werk van roest bikken uit de stalen dekken. Het spoelen van de luiken werd nooit gedaan met brak of zout water omdat het de lading zou kunnen bederven en het ijzer zou kunnen aantasten, nee alleen vers schoon water voor het spoelen werd gebruikt dat rechtstreeks uit de zoetwaterkanalen werd gepompt. Piet en zijn jongere broers stonden altijd vroeg op. In de zomer hadden ze ontbijt van Francines zelfgebakken brood met roomboter en kaas en zelfgemaakte aardbeienjam en dronken er thee bij. Na het ontbijt moest de dauw van de luiken gespoeld worden. Het is slecht voor de teer zeiden ze, maar ik denk dat dat slechts een excuus is om ze vroeg uit bed te krijgen, tienerjongens zijn berucht omdat ze geen vroege vogels zijn.

Enkele dagen na het uitbreken van de oorlog op 10 mei 1940 lag de Scheldestroom in Walsoorden beladen met grote zware bomen. Zeilklaar, met als bestemming de Bruynzeel potloodfabriek in Zaandam nabij Amsterdam. Een goede zeilbries blies die middag de Scheldestroom in ongewoon snel tempo over de Westerschelde. Toen zij dichter bij de kleine haven van Hansweert kwamen waren ze plotseling en zonder waarschuwing getuige van hun eerste bombardement van de Tweede Wereldoorlog. De Stuka "duikbommenwerper" van de Luftwaffe met hun kriegspiel van gruwelijke gillende sirenes, bevestigd aan de vleugels om opzettelijk de bevolking te terroriseren en het moreel van de vijand te verzwakken, veroorzaakte massale angst door oorverdovend gehuil toen de Luftwaffe hun bommen liet vallen op de kanaalsluizen van Hansweert. Gelukkig vielen ze ver weg van de naderende Scheldestroom. Meteen verborg Francine uit voorzorg haar zoontjes Kees en Bram onder de zware dikke teakhouten tafel. Kees en Piet manoeuvreerden in rap tempo de Scheldestroom richting terug naar Walsoorden.

Toen ze alweer aankwamen op de kleine haven van Walsoorden konden ze niet geloven wat ze zagen. "Een beangstigende shemozzle van wanorde", zei Francine, die medelijden had met de aanwezige Belgische en Franse troepen die zo slecht en jammerlijk waren uitgerust met ouderwets materieel dat door paarden en hondenwagens getrokken werd en alleman, mens en dier in een volkomen staat van ongeorganiseerde paniek verkeerden. Gelukkig hielden Kees en Francien al hun zinnen bij elkaar. De Franse commandant zei dat de Scheldestroom de haven van Walsoorden moest blokkeren om te voorkomen dat de Duitsers daar zouden landen en gaf Kees de opdracht om de Scheldestroom midden in de haven te ankeren en dan zouden de Fransen het schip met dynamiet opblazen. Maar snel nadenkend en slim zei Kees in het Frans: *"Monsieur tu vois mon bateau est bordé de grands arbres il ne peut pas couler"*, vertaalde betekenis: *'meneer, u kunt zien dat mijn schip is geladen met grote zware bomen, het zal nooit zinken.* "Ja, dat zou het geval kunnen zijn", antwoordde de Franse commandant. Toen, in een flits, een aantal zeer luidruchtig "vol gas" met lawaai van enge sirenes. Met klonk doken de Luftwaffe Stuka's dreigend laag over de haven. Binnen enkele seconden verdampten de Franse en Belgische troepen, vluchtende, zonder de Scheldestroom op te blazen. "Gelukkig" zei Kees, "God is met ons deze keer".

Acht maanden voor de Duitse inval in Nederland vertelt Kees me dat Jan, hun oudste zoon die met Bets van der Hooft trouwde, in oktober 1939 werd gemobiliseerd om bij de Nederlandse marine te dienen. Op woensdag 15 mei 1940, de dag dat Nederland zich overgaf, vocht Zeeland door samen met de Britse Marine en 60.000 Franse en Belgische troepen die nog steeds in Zeeland vochten. Jan diende toen op een mijnenveger van de Nederlandse marine, eigenlijk was het een omgebouwde vissersboot die mijnen opruimde op de Schelde. De Luftwaffe werd geobserveerd door andere schepen en ook de kustwacht meldden dat magnetische mijnen over de hele Westerschelde gestrooid waren. Op die noodlottige woensdag omstreeks 14.00 uur hebben vier Luftwaffe Stuka's het schip van de Nederlandse Marine met geweervuur gebombardeerd en besproeid, waarbij Jan ernstig gewond raakte, door granaatscherven in zijn buik. De vliegtuigen van de Luftwaffe keerden terug om hun bombardementsmissie tot een goed einde te brengen. Bij toeval vaarden de nabijgelegen Britse escorte-torpedobootjagers, *HMS Whitley* en *HMS Valentine*, die hun luchtdoelartillerie openden. Deze actie van de Britten redde het leven van de Nederlandse matrozen. Helaas, de bommen bedoeld voor het Nederlands schip troffen de Valentine om 14.30,Cdr. *Herbert James Buchanan*, de kapitein van de HMS Valentine, strandde zijn schip in zinkende toestand op een dijk vlak bij Terneuzen. De hele bevolking van Terneuzen rouwden. De opoffering van 31 bemanningsleden van de Valentine die omgekomen waren en nog eens 21 gewonden. Met veel pijn in het hart zei Francine, die de tranen van de liefde van een moeder toonde, dat ze hun lieve Jan in januari 1941 verloren hadden door granaatscherven en een gebrek aan medische zorg, maar voegde er aan toe dat dr. van Breda Vriesman, in de volksmond genoemd *Bredaatje Vriesman*, er alles aan gedaan had wat mogelijk was. Niet alleen voor Jan maar ook voor de 21 gewonden die in het ziekenhuis in Terneuzen opgenomen waren. RIP oom Jan.

De zaken begonnen al snel te verslechteren nadat de Britse marine, Belgische en Franse troepen zich terugtrokken. Onlangs vond ik een oude krant. Kees werd geïnterviewd door "Het Vrije Volk". Een grote krant van na de oorlog. Betreffende het inbeslagneming van de Scheldestroom voor ombouw tot landingsvaartuig dat gebruikt zou worden voor een Duitse invasie naar Engeland over de Noord Zee.

*"In 1940, na het lossen van een lading bomen in Rotterdam, kwam Paulusse terug in Terneuzen toen de Duitsers hem bevolen terug te keren naar Rotterdam, een sleepboot stond al klaar om de taak uit te voeren en snel de Scheldestroom terug naar Rotterdam te slepen. Eenmaal in Rotterdam beloofde Paulusse een groep verlaten uitziende Belgische schippers wier schepen in beslag waren genomen en beloofden hen: "Als ik mijn schip kan behouden, zal ik jullie gratis naar huis brengen. De Duitsers vonden de Scheldestroom niet geschikt om naar Engeland te varen, en dus kon Paulusse zijn belofte nakomen, en hij bracht de gedupeerde Belgen met hun goederen en bezittingen naar hun kustadressen. Het ging hier om zes gezinnen.*

The Scheldestroom is being towed from Terneuzen to Rotterdam organised by the Nazis who wanted to convert her to a landing craft. De Scheldestroom word weg gesleept over de Schelde naar Rotterdam waar de Duitsers he in beslag wouden nemen.

Toen de nazi's in Europa zegevierden, vestigden de Nederlandse economie zich bijna als normaal onder de bezetting. Deze economische pauze zou snel veranderen. Kees zei dat iedereen, mannelijk vrouwelijk en beest, machines en handel, zelfs de hele Nederlandse overheidsbureaucratie werkte voor de Duitsers inclusief de Scheldestroom, er was geen keus. De beperking kwam al snel, het luisteren naar de radio was verboden door de Duitsers. Al vlug waren er razzia's speciaal voor radio's en fietsen in beslag te nemen zonder betaling of compensatie. Rantsoenkaarten fungeerden als betaalmiddel tegen de winstgevende zwarte markt.

Keer op keer vlogen de jachtvliegtuigen van de RAF en schoten op alles wat voer in de Schelde. De Duitse aanvoerlijn was het doelwit van RAF-gevechtsvliegtuigen. Wonder boven wonder is er niemand gedood op de Scheldestroom, met uitzonderingen dat af en toe granaatscherven dekken en luiken beschadigden, maar er waren nooit een dode gevallen. De Scheldestroom was een ' lucky ship ' De Duitsers ruimden voortdurend de Magnetische zeemijnen op die continue gedropt werden bij de Royal Airforce. Toch bleef Francine zich zorgen maken over haar van Aalst-zussen Leine en Marie, beiden getrouwd met schippers, haar zorgen waren niet ongegrond. Het drama sloeg toe toen Leine's echtgenoot Bram tijdens het zeilen met zijn schip er een luchtgevecht tussen de Luftwaffe en de RAF boven zijn schip plaats vond. "Een granaatscherf trof hem, arme Bram en arme Leine", zei Francine. Drie meisjes en hun moeder waren achter gebleven. RIP oom Bram van Hanegem.

Gedurende de vijf jaar oorlog werd voedsel dringend schaars. Veel van de Zeeuwse landbouwproducten waren bestemd voor Duitsland ten koste van de Nederlandse burgers. Kees steelde een deel van dit voedsel illegaal, "van de moffen", zei hij, "om hongerige Nederlanders te voeden." Mijn vader Piet had zijn eigen weg in de voedseldistributie. Toen hij als 16-jarige teenager de losgiek van de Scheldestroom bediende, hangend met een net vol aardappelen. Dit werd gretig gadegeslagen door hongerige Rotterdamse kinderen die klaar stonden om de er uit gevallen aardappelen heel snel op te rapen zonder te worden opgemerkt door het wakend oog van de NSB-inspecteur in zijn belachelijk zwarte gekreukeld pakje. Piet, manipuleerde de losgiek zó dat het schudde en meer aardappelen uit het net vielen op de loopplank en tussen het dek van de Scheldestroom. Piet riep naar de kinderen om snel aan boord te komen en de gemorste aardappelen op te rapen. Binnen een seconde waren er ongeveer twintig kinderen aan boord om hunzelf te helpen.

De verachtelijke NSB'er (Nationaal-Socialistische Beweging) die optrad als een pseudo-politiemacht en altijd samenwerkte met de vijand sprong aan boord de Scheldestroom en beveelde de kinderen van het schip af te gaan. Dat was genoeg voor Piet om, "deze vuile NSB'er" van de Scheldestroom te donderen. Er ontstond een hevige maar opzettelijke woordenwisseling tussen Piet en de NSB'er om de kinderen de tijd te geven om de vele gevallen aardappelen op te rapen. Er ging geen liefde verloren tussen de NSB'ers en de echte Zeeuwen.

De NSB'er, wat te verwachten is van een landverrader, had de Gestapo-officieren gealarmeerd en binnen 30 minuten werd Piet gearresteerd en naar de nazi Sicherheitspolizei in Rotterdam gebracht. Kees kwam 30 minuten later terug omdat hij nieuwe lading had veiliggesteld en een vrachtmanifest had opgesteld. Hij was zich van niets bewust van wat er had plaats gevonden. Francine vertelde het verhaal en spoorde Kees aan om met de chef van de Gestapo te gaan praten die hij eerder in Rotterdam had ontmoet toen de Duitsers de Scheldestroom in beslag wilden nemen, die toen gelukkig ongeschikt bleek te zijn voor de invasie van Engeland.

Kees gebruikte zijn beste psychologie omdat hij wist dat fanatici en fascisten worden gedreven door een misplaatst en gemakkelijk gekneusd ego en ze zich graag superieur voelen. Er werd geen tijd verspild door Piet zijn excuses te laten aan bieden aan de NSB'er en tegelijkertijd vertelde Kees tegen de Gestapo-chef dat zijn 16 jarige zoon aan een geestelijk kwaal en aan een psychische aandoening leed en dat hij hem streng zou straffen. Het ego van de NSB'er en de Gestapo werd gemasseerd en gevoed; Kees bood opnieuw zijn excuses aan en Piet werd zonder meer vrijgelaten. Opgelucht keerden ze terug naar de Scheldestroom. Kees legde Piet natuurlijk uit dat zijn optreden allemaal maar toneel spelen was en niets er van waar was, want als hij niet zo had gepresteerd zou het een verblijf in een nazi-revalidatiekamp in Vucht zijn geweest voor de jonge driftige Piet.

Opa Paulusse in een 1959 gesprek met "de Vrije Zeeuw" de krant van Terneuzen:

> *"We meerden af in de jachthaven van Terneuzen ik zei tegen "grootje" (zoals hij zijn vrouw noemde tegenover zijn familie en ons kinderen) "de moffen staan al op de Schepen-dijk met een paar vrachtwagens die alles stelen wat los en vast staat, vooral koper en bron. Ik gaf opdracht aan de jongens om heel snel de grote bronzen scheepsbel van de Scheldestroom overboord te sodemieteren en ook het Philips-Punt radiootje want de Gestapo doet pietluttige zoektochten. De jongens Kees, Piet en Bram konden duiken om alles later weer uit het water te vissen. De radio stond op een geheime plek in de Roef verstopt in een valse kast, de*

De Art Deco Philips-puntradio was het eerste die uit het water gevist
werd. Wij hadden deze radio in 1961 meegenomen naar Australië waar
hij nog steeds speelt na 90 jaar. Toen maakten ze dingen om lang mee
te gaan voordat een door de consument aangedreven economie die
ingebouwde veroudering van alle dingen introduceerde.

Begin 1942 vroeg schoondochter Bets, die nog steeds rouwde om het
overlijden van haar man Jan-Pieter, aan Kees en Francine om drie joden,
een moeder en twee jongens, te helpen verbergen op de Scheldestroom.
Ze herinnerden zich dat Kees tijdens de economische depressie een
geheime ruimte had gebouwd om voedsel op te slaan dat de Nederlandse
regering had gestolen en Kees had gered van beschamende vernietiging.
Bets merkte ook op dat een van de joodse metaalhandelaars met de
naam Cracau, in Terneuzen, Kees om toevlucht had gevraagd op de
Scheldestroom.

Kees luisterde aandachtig toen Bets zei dat haar joodse buurman, een
heel lief jongetje genaamd *Victor Walg* die op de Van Steenberglaan
51 woonde (Bets woonde op nummer 57), ernstig gevaar liep om
gedeporteerd te worden. Zij had opgemerkt dat één van de Terneuzens
NSB'ers rond hun huis hing en het gaf haar een onheilspellend gevoel.
Ze smeekte Kees bijna om drie leden van de familie Walg korte tijd
onder te laten duiken op de Scheldestroom. Kees stemde er mee in.

Hun geheime plek was klaar. Ze wachtten en helaas nog eens wachtten, maar ze kwamen niet.

Tot grote ontsteltenis van alle buren aan de van Steenberglaan, deporteerden de Duitsers begin maart 1942 de familie Walg naar Amsterdam, helaas te laat om zich te kunnen verschuilen op de Scheldestroom. Het trieste was dat op 3 september 1942 ze naar het Nederlandse doorgangskamp Westerbork werden gestuurd en de volgende dag vertrok de hele arme familie Walg met het transport naar Auschwitz. Victor en zijn twee broertjes, zijn mama en papa … heel deze Joodse familie noodlottig vermoord in Auschwitz op 7 september 1942. Het raakte mij altijd als tante Bets mij als kind lieve verhalen vertelde van het joodse jongetje van mijn leeftijd en zijn broertjes met wie ze af en toe ging wandelen en zeilen met modelzeilboten, speciaal gebouwd door opa Paulusse voor jongens om mee te spelen. Tante Bets en haar verhalen maakten een diepe impact op mij, mijn spiritualiteit en de manier waarop ik de wereld mijn hele leven heb bekeken. Voor jaren werkten tante Bets in het badhuis in Terneuzen. Iedereen noemde haar "Betsie" en niet veel mensen wisten van haar verdriet, want ze was altijd opgewekt en vrolijk.

In september 1944 was er een zeer jonge Duitse soldaat genaamd Werner, nog geen 18 jaar oud, die zich had verstopt tussen het zeil van de Scheldestroom. Hij zat daar te kreunen van de koorts, zoals Francine zei, *'t ventje had zware griep en de moffen zouden hem onmiddellijk neerschieten op verdenking dat hij zijn post zou hebben verlaten.* Dr Bredaatje Vriesman werd geroepen om naar Werner te kijken. Francine ontfermde zich over deze jonge Duitse soldaat." 'tis zonde" zei ze, "dat arm ventje, 't moest je eigen zoon maar zijn". Werner werd door Piet en Kees verstopt in de geheime plaats in het de "foc's'ole" van de Scheldestroom waar het warm was tussen de reserve, zeilen, touw en teer. Kees zei keer op keer in gesprekken dat oude mannen,de politici, onschuldige en onwetende jonge mannen er op uit stuurden om te vechten. Toen de Duitsers zich hadden teruggetrokken leverden Piet en broer Kees Werner af naar een punt in Terneuzen waar hij veilig werd overgebracht naar een krijgsgevangenenkamp.

Naarmate de bezetting voortduurde werd het in ieder geval voor Kees en Francien duidelijk dat de Duitsers niet wonnen, deze conclusie hadden ze getrokken uit het feit dat onophoudelijk 24/7 geallieerde bommissies naar Duitsland vlogen. Vaak over de Schelde, soms zo dicht naast elkaar dat de vliegtuigen de zon blokkeerden over Terneuzen. Ook de nazi's voelden een nederlaag op gang komen, je kon het ook zien aan hun grillige, onvoorspelbare en onlogische gedrag. Kees zei dat ze niet alleen hun arrogante zelfvertrouwen verloren hadden, maar ook hun moed. Ze toonden neerslachtigheid, tenminste als hun verwarde uiterlijk de maatstaf was. Wanhopig op zoek naar mankracht begonnen ze willekeurige razzia's en pikten nietsvermoedende mannen en jongens van soms nog geen veertien jaar uit de straten van Terneuzen op om als slaven te dienen voor de nazi-oorlogsmachine in Duitsland.

De Paulussen verstopten, samen met vele andere goede Terneuzenburgers, hun jongens Piet en Kees met 16 van hun vrienden. Francine herinnerde zich, *het was als een magische verdwijning act van Houdini, al onze jongens verdwenen van de straat in minder dan een nanoseconde* en voegde eraan toe dat de moffen en NSB'ers woedend en tastbaar waren. Ze werden via de Schelde vervoerd in drie houten zeilsloepen zonder motor. Over water was wel het meest veilig omdat de wegen zwaar bewaakt werden door de Duitsers en NSB'ers. Als ze gepakt zouden worden, zouden de jongens onmiddellijk ter plaatse worden geëxecuteerd, althans dat is wat de verklaringen van de sympathiserende nazi-burgemeester van Terneuzen zeiden.

Kees en zijn broer Bram en enkele andere schippers namen de leiding over de sloepen. Ze kenden de wateren van Terneuzen tot aan de Emmapolder en de ondergelopen landen van Safinghe als hun broekzak. Op verschillende punten langs de Schelde werden snel een paar jongens gelost en de Nederlandse ondergrondse bracht hen naar afgelegen boerderijen tot diep de polder in. Piet zou met een aantal anderen worden verstopt in een schaapskooi of scheerstal op de ondergelopen landen van Safinghe. Schipper Kees kende de weg in deze verraderlijke moerassen. Als kind ging hij erheen om verscheidene zeegroenten te oogsten, meer recent aan het begin van de oorlog toen hij een partij had geleid die waardevolle machineonderdelen van de veerboten die de Schelde bevoeren wegstaken zodat de Duitsers enkele van de veerboten niet konden gebruiken. Het verbaasde hem nog steeds dat hij nooit werd gevonden, dat de nazi's hem nooit ondervroegen naar de verblijfplaats van zijn jongens, niet echt verwonderlijk want de dagen waren waanzinnig vertoond zoals op dinsdag 5 september 1944. 'Dolle Dinsdag' angstige dagen met een verkapte zegen, vooral toen alle NSB'ers mijmerend vertrokken in een hoogst amusante en schofterige ontsnappingsgolf, waaronder de burgemeesters van Terneuzen en zijn bende medewerkers.

In die tijd waren er ook hevige gevechten in West-Zeeuws Vlaanderen waar de Duitsers 82.000 troepen hadden gestationeerd, die dijken hadden opgeblazen en grote delen zo onder water kwamen te staan waardoor de geallieerde opmars werd belemmerd. De Scheldestroom, met vele andere schepen, werd in Terneuzen opgeborgen toen de Canadezen en Poolse troepen de Duitsers uit Zeeuws Vlaanderen verdreven. Toen ze terugkwamen van de onderduik van hun jongens, doken Kees en vele andere schippers zelf onder. De Duitsers vorderden hun schepen om hen te helpen ontsnappen over de Schelde naar Vlissingen en eisten van de schippers dat ze ze over zouden varen, dit weigerden ze en doken onder. Kees met twee andere schippers was ondergedoken in Brugstraat 3, bij bakker Wisse in Othene. 'Noten' in de volks mond. Hij vertelde, "Maar wat zaten wij daar goed zeg achter de grote broodoven. Lekker warm ook, en wij mochten helpen in de bakkerij blikjes brood smeren, hout kappen voor de hele familie Wisse, tjonge wat hebben we daar veel worstenbroodjes gegeten". En ja, Francine was er ook goed mee weggekomen. Zij was bij haar moeder in de Javastraat want de havens waren onveilig en werden min of meer constant bestoken met kanonnenvuur. De hele familie van Aalst kreeg ook worstenbroodjes. Worst van paardenvlees gemaakt omdat er zoveel paarden zomaar los liepen werden er veel geslacht. Dus zodoende kreeg Francine gratis worstenbroodjes, bezorgd door de knecht van Wisse. Dus dat liedje van Bob Scholte," Breng eens een zonnetje… wie goed doet goed ontmoet, kwam uit. Iedereen behalve de NSB'ers werkten samen voor één doel:

# HOOFDSTUK 7

*De Thuiskoms van Gerrit Tanis Schipper uit*
*Terneuzen werd zwervende Onderduiker.*

Op de winteravonden kwamen de schippersfamilies, die naast elkaar of in de nabijheid gemeerd lagen, buurten en vertelden zij elkaar groote verhalen. De sfeer in de Roef van de Scheldestroom de perfecte plek voor hartelijke gesprekken en verhalen was, vermengd met de geur van zoete toffee, pijptabak of de aangename geur van sigaren en Francines vers gezette gepercoleerde pruttelkoffie. Om alvast in de stemming te komen werd er achtergrondmuziek gespeeld vanaf hun draagbare opwindbare grammofoon platenspeler met een uitgebreide collectie 78rmp platen. Ze betaalden er geen geld voor maar ruilden het "voor een grote zak aardappelen ergens in 'Olland', zei Francine, "want die arme stakkers stierven bijna van de grote vrete".

De familie kwam samen wanneer ze allemaal in dezelfde haven waren. Francines jongste zus Marie was getrouwd met Gerrit Tanis, een schipper van een binnenvaartolietanker de Nijverheid. Ze kwamen vaak op bezoek. Ome Gerrit was een meesterverteller, altijd intrigerend en vond zelfs in slechte situaties iets humoristisch. De andere factor van entertainment was de manier waarop hij de Nederlandse taal gebruikte. Schippers in Nederland spraken in een soort *schippers-taal* die soms beledigend kon zijn voor de gevoelige oren van kostbare prinsessen. Ik herinner me een avontuurlijk verhaal waarin hij zijn olietanker in het binnenland tot zinken bracht, die de Duitsers wanhopig wilden hebben. Het verhaal dat hij vertelde heette: De thuiskomst van Gerrit Tanis.

## De thuiskomst van Gerit Tanis

Met dolle dinsdag was ik in Antwerpen om mijn schip te anti
magnetiseren tegen mijnen. Als ik toen slim was geweest en ik had m'n
schip los gedonderd en ik was daar naar boven Antwerpen gelopen naar
Dendermonde, toen gebeurde het. s' Nachts moest ik naar beneden,
naar Hansweert. Daar zeiden de moffen dat ik naar Wilhelmshafen
moest. De vrouw was ook nog aan boord, ik zeg, maar daar ga ik niet
naar toe. Ik zeg tegen de vrouw... Jullie de wal op en die Nijverheid,
dat was mijn schip, die sneuvelt wel ergens onderweg. Die kom niet in
Whilhelmshafen, dat moeten ze niet denken. Afijn mijn vrouw aan
de wal met de kinderwagen en een koffertje en ik weg. In Hansweert
lag ook de Luxor. Het ouwe waterbootje van Terneuzen, daar zat mijn
broer op en er lag nog een schip van Oude Tonge. Wij met z'n drieën
over de Oosterschelde, alles vluchtte. En schieten en mitrailleren dat ze
deden ...potverju.., maar ja, wij geraakten in de tramhaven bij Zijpe, daar
hebben we een hele dag in de grond gezeten want d'r kwamen steeds
Engelse vliegtuigen over de Grevelingen en maar mitrailleren ...schieten
oppende Duitsers, want die vluchten met alles wat dreef, maar de één
zat daar aan de grond en de andere een dije verder. Dus dat was goed
schieten voor die mannen daar boven.

s'Avonds moesten we er uit. Dat ging niet makkelijk want de Duitsers
sprongen op elk schip wat wegvoer. Wij kregen er ook een paar mee.
Alles, we raakten buiten, maar bij Oude Tonge gooiden ze ons onder
een lichtkogel. We lagen met z'n drieën opzei van mekaar. De Luxor,
een vracht scheepje, de Nijverheid en allemaal lichtkogels. Zo dreven
wij ze aan de grond. Daarboven deden ze niks, geen eens een bom...
niks. Wij hadden vijf Duitsers aan boord, ik zeg tegen die Duitsers," ze
kunnen best magnetische mijne gegooid hebben. Als je daar op raakt
vlieg je ook de lucht in." We hebben besproken wat we moesten doen.
Ik zou naar Strijen varen. Ik dacht dan zet ik 'm daar aan de Moerdijk
wel ergens met z'n donder aan de grond. De tonnen waren weg. Maar
we gingen toch het keten in. We kwamen aan in Dinteloord toen
het net dag was. D'r was geen sterveling te zien, niks. We hebben es

afgewacht, maar er gebeurde niks. D'r stond een mitrailleur, daar kon je zo de kogels vinden, alles er bij. Die armen die daar hadden gezeten waren 'm allemaal gepleit. Niks meer te bekennen. De Duitsers die bij mij aan boord waren gingen in een loopgraaf slapen. Ik heb toen wat spulletjes gepakt en wat kleren. Tegen de andere mannen hebben we gezegd dat we om boodschappen gingen, melk en zo. Dat was goed. "Kom maar terug als het donker is." Wij weg. Toen zijn wij ergens in een polder in een boerenhoeven gekropen, die stond onder water. Het was de Herkingse polder, bij Stampersgat.

Dat water stond al hoog. Toen we daar een dag of drie inzaten zijn we er uit gemoeten omdat we niks te eten hadden. s'Nachts kropen we in de bomen van de Boogerd om een appeltje te zoeken. We hadden nog een potje augurkjes gevonden, maar we zaten er met ons zessen. Daar moet je niet min over denken. Wij zijn er blijven zitten, veertien dagen lang op een schuurzolder. We sliepen op stro. Dat hadden we uit de schelf gehaald, maar luizen dat er zaten, jonge..jonge luízen… je werd helemaal rot gevreten. Je haar nat maken en dan met een kam er door. t'Was net een dierentuin op je kop.

Op een morgen zitten we daar. Het was stormensweer geweest. O ja, dat moet ik je nog vertellen. We hadden een boek kaarten bij ons. We zitten daar te kaarten op dat eiland en daar horen we ineens de buitendeur. Hé, wat is dat…m'n broer springt naar de zoldertrap en die ziet net een vent weggaan, de deur was weer dicht. Hij doet de deur open… er staat een boer buiten. Die man vraagt, "wat zitten jullie hier te doen?" We vertelden dat we ondergedoken waren. Hij zegt, "ik kom hier om de schuurdeur dicht te doen want die is opengewaaid." We wisten dat wel maar ja, wij kwamen niet beneden als het niet nodig was en niet buiten ook, want daar verzoop je. Hij zegt, "ik kan niks voor je doen, ik heb hier Joden gehad maar ik wil nu geen rottigheid meer." Van die Joden dat is waar want die zolder was zo gemaakt dat je achter een paar plankjes nog een heel verblijf had. Daar hadden we die augurkjes gevonden en ook nog een petroliestel. Wij hadden het zo omgebouwd dat we er in konden vluchten als er Duitsers zouden komen.

Die boer kon niks doen, dus daar zaten we. s 'Avonds om een uur of negen werd er geklopt. We dachten die vuile boer heeft ons verraden. Niks hoor, is het zijn broer met zo'n grote 12 liter melkkan, drie tarwebroden en een pond boter. Toen waren we al een heel eind op pad eej. Nou was er bij ons eentje van Oude Tonge, die was goed bekent in die polder. Hij zegt op een morgen, "ik zal op verkenning gaan." Hij de polder in. Hij komt daar met ene Bousche van Breskens in aanraking. Die zat daar op een woonboot weggestoken. Z'n schip was op de Braakman gezonken. Hij zegt, "zal jullie eens een ketel met pee, en met Juun koken." Dat deed ie, en die bracht dat.

's avonds naar ons toe. Zo scharrelden we een beetje weg eej. Toen kwamen die rot vliegtuigen op een zondagmorgen. We wisten niet wat er was want je dust niet buiten te komen. D'r zaten ook Zweefvliegtuigen bij...nou raakt er eentje los en dondert zo achter in de tuin in het water. Je kon er niet naar toe want dan verzoop je. Ja toen had je het zitten. We verwachtten elk moment de Moffen, maar ze kwamen niet. Dat vliegtuig, we wisten dat het er lag, maar je zag niks. s 'Morgens ben ik er met die Oude Tongenaar naar gegaan. s' Morgens om vier uur. Ik dacht, "als ze er komen, dan zijn wij er aan." Dus wij weg.

Naar de weg en gaan kijken. We kwamen bij een boertje in een ander polder, die zaten te eten. D'r zat daar binnen zoveel ongedierte dat je zijn ogen niet zag van de vliegen. Een huishouden nog nooit zo gezien, maar we mogen mee-eten. t 'Was een echte Brabander. We kregen er een beetje inlichtingen en wij weer weg. Wij komen aan, staan daar buiten bij ene Scheele. Die kwam feitelijk van Axel. Hij zat in de ondergrondse. Toen we er kwamen was hij er niet, z'n vrouw wel. Ze maakten eten voor ons klaar. We vertelden waar we zaten. Ze zei dat ze zou proberen wat voor ons te doen. Nou, en zo moesten we weer zoeken om naar ons vogelnest in de polder te komen. Die jongens daar verwachten ons s 'avonds weer terug. Dus wij terug. Bij Standaard-buiten komen we een boerenknecht tegen met een stel paarden. "Ho!" zegt ie, "Stap maar op." Wij mee en die vent met ons op stap. t' Standaard-buiten... voor het gemeentehuis. "Hier moeten we een inbraak plegen" zegt ie tegen mij. Allez, we komen daar binnen. D'r zaten nog drie ambtenaren. "Hoeveel broodkaarten moeten jullie hebben, hoeveel bonnen?" 't Was zo geregeld. "Vannacht komen we jullie halen", zeg één van die lui. Die man met z'n boerenwagen wou ons terug brengen. Ik zeg, "dat gaan we niet doen. We zoeken zelf wel terug te geraken."

Nee, dat kon niet met zo'n wagen door dat water naar de hoeve. Dan weet iedereen gelijk waar we zitten. Ik zeg, en we komen er zelf wel uit ook. Als we maar weten waar we naar toe moeten. Dus wij terug naar die jongens. We vertelden heel de situatie. De volgende morgen om een uur of zes kwamen er twee mensen met lieslaarzen aan. Eén heette 'van Dis', ze kwamen zeggen dat we s' avonds daar en daar naartoe moesten. Dat hebben we te voet gedaan. Dan zijn wij naar een school gegaan. Daar hadden ook mannen van de Duitsers gezeten, daar waren bedden, dekens, potten en pannen. Die hebben wij er uitgehaald. Daar in Fijnaart kwamen we terecht, aan de nieuwe molen. Daar was een aardappelmagazijn, er stond een kachel in en aardappelkisten. We hebben er een hele kamer van gemaakt en wat kribben er in gezet. Wij hebben daar twee maanden in geleefd en gewerkt bij een boer. We hebben geoogst, geslacht en we hebben de pee uitgedaan en de aardappelen. Die boer zei, "jullie kunnen alles." Ja, allicht dat ie tevree was. M'n broer had heel z'n keuken geplakt en geschilderd. Die boer had dertig fuiken. Ik ging er mee vissen. Wij zijn er gebleven tot de bevrijding gekomen is. Dan ben ik naar huis gegaan in Terneuzen.

Maar onderweg stond ik in Baarland en ik kon niet verder want Jan Jongman en Klaasje Quellerri voeren niet meer. Daarvoor deden ze het stiekem met een Hoogaarsje want toen later werd de Schelde verboden.

Er dreven te veel mijnen. Potverdorie wat nu? Daar was een hoop volk daar aan Baarland, maar niemand kon over. Nou, Zandaardappel de commandant van de Schelde-wacht, die zat in het huis van de havenmeester. Er was ook een vrouw bij met een kind van Tholen, d'r man, zat op een mijnenveger. Die had vijf jaar in Engeland gezeten maar lag nou mijnen te vegen voor Terneuzen. Dat mens wou naar d'r man maar ze kon ook niet over geraken. Ze kende wel die wachtsman. Nou komt die vent naar me toe...Hij zegt "jij bent schipper eej? Durf jij met de pijlboot naar Terneuzen te roeien?" Ik zeg ja, dat durf ik wel. Maar één ding… er mag niet te veel volk in die boot want die boot raakt overladen en allemaal verzuipen dat kan niet. En weet je, als die boot klaar lig, dan springen ze er allemaal in. En ik kan ze er niet uit houden want ze hebben net zo veel recht als ik. "Daar zorg ik voor", zegt de commandant. Afijn het ging allemaal goed maar we waren nog geen vijfhonderd meter buiten de haven of daar komen die mijnenvegers uit Terneuzen af. BSS mijnenvegers, van die grote vlammen uit het water. Ja, waar moet je dan naar toe met z'n roeiboot vol met volk. t 'Was ebbe dus wij varen de Everdingen op naar Borsele, gaat het nog een keer waaien ook… een dikke bries de ebbe d'r in een berg zee.

Dat kind was al zeeziek. We hadden het in dekens gerold, maar t' zat al te spoegen. t' Was een kind van een jaar of acht. Ik zeg "jongens, als we maar overkomen. We moeten een beetje water er uit scheppen en dan komen we er wel. Als we maar tegen de wal raken van 't schip af en de dijk op." Met de vloed komen we eindelijk over aan De Eendracht oostelijk van Terneuzen. Ja jonge… dwars over de Westerschelde geroeid tussen de zand banken en al die mijnen met al die mensen, dat is wat hoor. "Schipper nou zijn wij ver genoeg" zeiden die mensen toen ze de dijk zagen. Ik zeg "nee, we moeten verder naar het laatje van de Griete want aan die dijk komen jullie er nooit uit. Als we met de boot tegen de stenen aan komen verzuipen we allemaal. Die boot wordt er tegen aan gedonder door de golven." Dus we roeiden kort onder de diek verder en geraken zo aan de Griete. Toen moesten we nog naar huis. Die van de PZEM hebben die meegenomen op de fiets naar Terneuzen. Ik ben gaan lopen naar Terneuzen over het Axelse bruggetje en het straatje bij ons in, net op 't schemer.

Onze Janna stond buiten. Ze roept: "Daar hebt je papa."

Ik was weer thuis

# HOOFSTUK 8

*Francine had alweer een zak aardappelen geruild voor een nieuw
Singer-naaimachine, zoals ze bij een andere gelegenheid ook deed.
Een zak met aardappelen omruilen voor een Phillips Point-radio.*

Maandag 13 maart 1945 "Kees! Waar op aarde heb je de zes meter lange oranje wimpel verstopt die ik gemaakt had voor het huwelijk van prinses Juliana? Ik kan het niet vinden." Francine kon haar opwinding niet verbergen toen een radiobulletin zojuist aankondigde dat koningin Wilhelmina (het symbool van het verzet) de Nederlandse grens overstak bij Eede, een dorp dertig kilometer gelegen van Terneuzen. Ze zou eerst een bezoek brengen in het oosten van Zeeuws-Vlaanderen, om troost te offeren aan de getroffene oorlogsslachtoffers van de catastrofaals verwoesting ter plaatse. De vele overstroomde polderdorpen en steden zoals Breskens, gelegen aan de ingang van het Schelde-estuarium, werden de dupe van het geallieerde offensief. "Over de oranje wimpel!" riep Francine de tweede keer: "Oh, ik herinner me de moffen, scheurden onze driekleurenvlag kapot tijdens het koper- en brons razzia. Maar niet de wimpel, die hebben ze gelukkig niet gevonden. We hadden het verborgen samen met de radio." Kees reageerde niet terwijl hij bezig was met het repareren van de luiken die zwaar beschadigd waren door grote granaatscherven van het afweergeschut, blijkbaar deed hij vaak alsof hij doof was als hij zich concentreerde op de taken die voorhanden lagen. Hij schrok op toen Francine zei dat ze een intuïtief gevoel had dat: 'Willemientje', een innemende koosnaam voor koningin Wilhelmina, s' morgens dinsdag 14 maart in Terneuzen zou aankomen.

Juist op dat moment kwamen haar jongste broer Hendrik en zijn vrouw Marie aan. Hun café in Sluiskil was plat gebombardeerd, ze logeerden nu bij zijn bejaarde moeder. Ze waren de Java-buurt uitgelopen met drie bouten stof. Rood, wit en blauw materiaal om de Nederlandse vlag te maken. Ook Tante Leine baant zich een weg met extra sterke garen die ze tijdens de oorlog bewaard had. Francine had alweer een zak aardappelen geruild voor een nieuw Singer-naaimachine, zoals ze bij een andere gelegenheid ook deed. Een zak met aardappelen omruilen voor een Phillips Point-radio.

Hun opwinding en opgewektheid steeg toen de vlag zijn rechthoekige vorm aannam samen met andere oranje vlaggetjes die allen over de gehele Scheldestroom wapperden. Ondertussen genoten alle vlaggenmakers van Francines zelfgemaakte vervangkoffie en spritzkoekjes die Hendrik had gebakken. Alle aanwezigen neurieden 'Het Wilhelmus', sommigen probeerden het hardop te zingen na vijf jaar het niet te hebben gezongen. Onder de bezetting kon men in een concentratiekamp belanden maar nu waren ze opgelucht dat ze alles konden zingen wat ze maar wilden waaronder het oudste volkslied ter wereld. Later hoorden ze over de radio dat de Terneuzenaren hartelijk en met volle emotie voor Willemientje zongen en feedback gaf dat ze het geweldig vond." Oranje boven!" Tranen van vreugde en verdriet vloeiden.

Dinsdag 13 maart om 19.00 uur hees Kees en Francine de zes meter lange oranje wimpel en de zelfgemaakte rood-wit-blauwe vlag hoog in de mast van de Scheldestroom. Weer was Francines intuïtie goed, de koningin komt eraan, de inwoners van dorpen en steden kregen slechts 60 minuten voor haar aankomst bericht. Het nieuws reisde snel van huis tot huis, van stadsomroeper naar burgers.

Om veiligheidsredenen mochten ze de Scheldestroom niet verlaten. Alle schepen die opgelegd waren, wapperden overal met enthousiasme de vlaggen van de bevrijders: Poolse, Britse, Canadese, Franse, Belgische en Amerikaanse vlaggen. De driekleur die die dag genaaid was op de Scheldestroom heb ik nog en ik zie dat de mot er ingezeten heeft.

Toch is er ook veel verdriet voor de Scheepvaartgemeenschap toen op Dolle Dinsdag 5 september 1944 vijf medewerkers van Rijkswaterstaat gruwelijk door de Duitsers werden geëxecuteerd voor het verwijderen van dynamiet uit de sluizen en bruggen rond Terneuzen. Iedereen in de scheepvaartgemeenschap kende deze dappere mannen persoonlijk omdat het sluiswachters en wateringenieurs waren die de toegang tot het zeekanaal Gent Terneuzen onderhielden en dienden. Ze waren professioneel, beleefd en behulpzaam voor de duizenden schippers die elk jaar door hun sluizen gingen. Hun namen zouden niet snel worden vergeten, twee wateringenieurs *Groenewegen* en *Hoolsema* en drie van de sluiswachters *De Bert*, *Verbrugge* en *Nieuwenhuize*. Wilhelmina zou later hun weduwen ontmoeten.

De favoriete neef van Francine en Kees, Ko Paulusse (een fotograaf), was op weg naar het dorpsplein '*de Mart*' om Hare Majesteit te verwelkomen. Hij verlegde zijn route naar zijn tante en oom voor koffie en spritz en een praatje in de altijd gezellige Scheldestroom Roef. Ko hoorde dat ze hun schip niet konden verlaten en stemde ermee in om foto's te maken en daarna zou hij met hen lunchen en verslag uitbrengen.

Onlangs in het jaar 2019, vlak voor Ko's tweeënnegentigste verjaardag, werd hij geïnterviewd door een krant waar hij herinneringen ophaalde aan het moment waarop hij drie meter van Koningin Wilhelmina stond: *De koningin was zichtbaar geraakt door de executie van deze onschuldige mannen, en ik hoorde haar duidelijk zeggen in die vreselijke executieplaats bij de westelijke sluis: "We moeten op deze plek een monument bouwen om deze moedige mannen te eren'.* En zo gebeurde het dat er een indrukwekkend monument werd gebouwd.

Zeeuws-Vlaanderen, het laatste gebied van Nederland dat zich overgaf en de eerste dat werd bevrijd. Toch luidde deze bevrijding voor de natie persoonlijke turbulentie in voor de Paulusse familie, een soort angst die ze nog niet eerder hadden ervaren. Dat ze hun oudste zoon Jan-Pieter al verloren hadden, is al erg genoeg, maar nu liepen al hun zonen het risico om bij de Nederlandse marine en in het leger te dienen.

Op de dag van het bezoek van de koningin was hun derde zoon Kees toevallig in Terneuzen op een Nederlands marineschip. Zijn oudere broer Piet is al ergens in Duitsland bij de geallieerden toegevoegd. Op 29 september 1944 was de dag dat Zeeuws-Vlaamse jonge mannen zich vrijwillig aansloten bij het Bataljon Zeeland I-14R.I. het eerste officiële Nederlands bataljon dat actief was bij de bevrijding. Bram, hun jongste, pas 17 jaar oud, zit al in de Nederlandse marine en nu zijn zowel hij als Kees samen met meer dan duizend andere jonge Nederlanders op weg naar het Oosten samen met bondgenoten om de Japanners te verslaan.

*Francine voelde een zwaar hart vanaf het moment dat haar jongens voor de laatste keer hun huis in de Scheldestroom verlieten, meer een kwelling van geest, het type dat ze nog niet eerder had meegemaakt. Nu zitten al haar zoons verbonden in het levensbedreigende oorlogstheater. Dit was niet het soort vrijheid dat ze verwachtte, ze besefte nu dat de natie meer offers van vele moeders eiste.*

Kees meer stoïcijns en dingen voor zichzelf probeerde te houden, kon het maar net redden. Maar ook zijn hart deed pijn, duidelijk door zijn meer dan frequente slokjes van zijn eigen gedistilleerde Citroen Jenever. Francine noemde het 'zijn citroentje voor troost'. Dit soort drank staat bekend als een uitstekend kalmerend middel, net zo goed als de huidige *Prozac* of *Valium*, het kalmeerde de geest. Ik herinner me deze jenever nog goed, vooral de grote lengte van de citroen pel die ondergedompeld lag in de doorzichtige gele jenever dat op een aantrekkelijk kunstwerk leek, iets dat je wilt proeven en ervaren. De citroengeur was verleidelijk zoet en warm. Na mijn constante gezeur om een teugje gaven ze toe en als zesjarige was het mijn eerste en laatste smaak van gele jenever. O, ik weet het nu zeker, ze gebruikten het als kalmeringsmiddel. In de weekenden dat vrienden op de koffie kwamen werden ze altijd begroet met 'wil je eerst een citroentje voor de koffie.' Dat aanbod was zo beminnelijk dat zelfs geheelonthouders het niet konden weerstaan.

Kees en zijn collega-schippers traden op als loods voor de geallieerden en hielp bij het markeren van de locaties op maritieme kaarten met verraderlijke zandbanken op de Schelde en de Braakman-estuaria. Francine en Leine dienden de geallieerden met vertaling voor het Engels en Nederlands verzorgenden. Bakker Wisse van Noten droeg ook bij met het eten voeren van alle soldaten. Zoals hij zei, "die ons weer vrijheid gaven" en leverde honderd worstenbroodjes gemaakt voor alle bemanning op de Scheldestroom. Maar geen mocht vertellen, vooral niet tegen de Canadezen of de Britten, dat er paardenvlees in de worstenbroodjes zat. Ze zouden walgen van het idee om paarden te eten. Eén van de Britse officieren die aan boord kwam voor vertaaldiensten was luitenant George Penney, een lang verloren gewaande penvriend van Francine die ze twintig jaar geleden ontmoette in het vluchtelingenkamp Hontenisse toen George werd geïnterneerd in een Nederlands militair bijzettingskamp waar hij heimwee had gehad. De zusters van Aalst hadden hem en een paar Engelse jongens geadopteerd en hielden contact tot het midden van de jaren dertig, een tijd om herinneringen op te halen. Het is altijd goed om een feest van nostalgie te hebben als lang verloren vrienden elkaar weer ontmoeten.

# SCHELDESTROOM NAWOORD

Het einde van de oorlog bracht geen verlichting noch gemoedsrust voor Francine en Kees. Hun dagen van onrust namen toe. Er was ook een tekort aan arbeidskrachten. Kees 'oudere broer, de 76-jarige Bram, wiens schip "Elizabeth" in beslag werd genomen door de nazi's, ging weer aan het werk als matroos op de Scheldestroom.

Zodra Zeeuws-Vlaanderen in september 1944 werd bevrijd, boden de overgebleven drie jongens zich vrijwillig aan voor de Nederlandse marine en het leger om de geallieerden te ondersteunen bij hun opmars naar Duitsland. Na de Duitse capitulatie werden de drie zoons naar Nederlands-Indië gestuurd om de Japanners te helpen verslaan. Kees en Francien waren *Zeeuws stoïcijns* ondanks hun voortdurende zorgen; in hun achterhoofd waren ze de Slag om de Javazee niet vergeten. Waar meer dan 2.300 Nederlandse en geallieerde zeelieden hun jonge leven verloren.

De familie Paulusse had, net als vele andere families, een aandeel in de toekomst van Nederland. Ze bleven op de hoogte van de politieke en economische ontwikkelingen door middel van lezen en discussies. Ze waren nooit een oppervlakkig stel dat hun geest versterkte door kritisch na te denken; bijgevolg werden ze zelden afgeschrikt door de wisselvalligheid van het leven. Francine kocht en las elk boek dat werd gepubliceerd over het werk en de vooruitgang die Bataljon Zeeland (2-14R.I.) in Nederlands-Indië verrichten. Deze boeken stonden vol met foto's van nieuwe ziekenhuizen, voedseldistributiecentra, transportschepen vol met *rōmusha's* en Nederlandse en geallieerde krijgsgevangenen, die terug naar Indonesië hun geboorte land werden gevaren.

Het idee dat hun jongens humanitair werk deden sprak hen aan, in plaats van een oorlog te voeren. Het was waar dat hun jongens niet in Indonesië waren om de koloniale status te behouden. Nederlandse troepen in Indonesië waren druk bezig de miljoenen rōmusha's terug te brengen naar Indonesië, de dwangarbeiders die de collaborateur Soekarno aan de Japanners had geleverd. De rechtsstaat moest worden toegepast. Britse en Nederlandse troepen bevrijdden de Japanse interneringskampen met duizenden Nederlandse vrouwen en hun kinderen. Nadat de Japanners zich hadden overgegeven werden deze geïnterneerden door de Indonesische Republikeinen tot losgeld gehouden. De Indonesische bevolking had weinig voedsel en de Nederlanders brachten voedsel, medische benodigdheden en herbouwde ziekenhuizen. Hun vermoeden van humanitair werk werd ondersteund door VN-statistieken. In een VN-rapport staat dat 4 miljoen mensen in Indonesië zijn omgekomen als gevolg van de Japanse bezetting. Ongeveer 2,4 miljoen mensen stierven op Java door hongersnood in 1944-45.

Het plan was dat ze snel met pensioen zouden gaan en zoon Piet de Scheldestroom zou kopen als hij terugkwam uit de oorlog. Hij kwam in 1948 terug uit Indonesië terwijl zijn broers Kees en Bram tot 1950 in dat strijdtoneel bleven. Geen van de jongens wilde de Scheldestroom bevaren, ze was te veel werk. Ook de toekomstige vrouwen en vriendinnen van Kees en Piet wilden geen schippersvrouwen zijn. In 1949 werd besloten om de Scheldestroom te verkopen. De nieuwe eigenaren behielden de naam Scheldestroom en verlengde haar met ongeveer 5 meter. Ze werd omgebouwd tot een motorschip.

Kees en Francine gingen officieel met pensioen door twee huizen te kopen in de Dahliastraat in Terneuzen. Eén huis verhuurden ze voor een pensioeninkomen omdat ze niet in aanmerking kwamen voor een door de overheid gefinancierd pensioen, de AOW, die zou later komen door Drees.

Op 16 juli 1957 verongelukte Bram, hun achtentwintigjarige zoon, in een KLM Super Constellation vlucht 844, die neerstortte in Cenderawasih Bay, 1,3 kilometer (0,75 mijl) van de vertrekluchthaven van Biak in voormalig Nederlands Nieuw-Guinea. Met als gevolg het verlies van 58 (waarvan 9 bemanningsleden) van de 68 mensen die aan boord waren. Hun hart brak verder toen Piet en zijn gezin in 1961 naar Australië migreerden. De migratie naar Australië staat beschreven in mijn boek Vertrek. Kees trouwde met Dolly en verhuisden naar Haarlem. Hun twee dochters, Janna en Bette, bleven in Terneuzen.

Het verleden blijft spreken en voor vele mensen vandaag is het een aanmoediging, zoals de bewaarde brieven en ansichtkaarten van lang geleden die mijn vier oma's en opa's, familie en vrienden mij hebben gestuurd. Deze ansichtkaarten en brieven zijn op fijn papier en mooi handschrift geschreven. Zelfs na decennia ruiken en voelen ze nog naar die tijd van de parfums en sigarengeur van dierbaren. Als ik me eenzaam voel herlees ik de positieve, schriftelijke bevestigingen op deze kaarten. Vooral die van mijn vele tantes en grootouders, die begonnen altijd met "lieve Kees" of "Darling Keith" Krachtige affirmaties die me door tijden van persoonlijke ontberingen en trauma's heen zagen. Blij dat ik die geschreven herinneringen in een schoenendoos bewaarde in plaats van dat ze nu digitaal rondzweven in de ether, versmolten en verloren met miljarden andere berichten.

Veertig jaar lang hadden ze gewoond en gedreven in de Scheldestroom. Varend op rivieren en zeeën, vaak tegen de wind in. De hunne was geen vaste woonwijk, maar toch kenden ze elke schippersfamilie alsof ze buren waren. De verandering was eeuwigdurend; er was zelden dezelfde locatie nog hetzelfde landschap. Elke dag kon er een storm gebeuren. Verandering zoals het weer was hun enige constante in het leven, aanpassen waar dan ook, was hun redder.

Nu trokken ze zich terug om permanent aan land te leven en te wonen. Een belangrijke gebeurtenis van overgang. Plots was er één huis in één buurt die, dag in dag uit, hetzelfde was. Ineens zagen Kees en Francine dezelfde buren iedere dag. Dat was nog de tijd waar een ieder zijn buren kenden. Toch hebben ze de ontmoeting met interessante mensen in hun nieuwe huis aan land niet gemist. Hun warme gastvrijheid trok een eindeloze variëteit aan boeiende bezoekers, vooral de internationale kopers van Kees' vintage modelschepen. Tegenwoordig hielden ze hun venster op wereldgebeurtenissen op het gebied van wetenschap, kunst en literatuur vast door het medium van tv.

Zij waren één van de eersten in Nederland die in 1952 een tv kochten. *"that's our new window to the world"*, zei Francine.

Francine stierf op 74 jarige leeftijd in 1962 van galblaascomplicaties. Ik bezocht Opa Kees in 1968, hij woonde gelukkig samen met z'n dochter Janna haar familie. Janna, jammer genoeg, stierf veel te vroeg op 48-jarige leeftijd. Op dat moment verhuisde Kees naar 'De Blide' een rusthuis in Terneuzen waar hij het uitstekend naar zijn zin had en waar nog andere schippers van zijn leeftijd woonden. Uit zijn brieven aan mij bleek dat hij van gezelligheid hield. Het is allemaal een kwestie van aanpassen, het enige constante in ons leven. Cornelis Paulusse stierf in 1972 op 86-jarige leeftijd.

De voetafdrukken van je voorouders zitten misschien in kunstwerken op ansichtkaarten en in het geval van de Paulusses is het de originele 110 jaar oude én nog varende Scheldestroom, zij is nog steeds bij ons. Mijn voorouders zijn niet dood. Men is pas goed dood als je vergeten bent.

Zij lieten hun voetafdrukken achter op de aarde; hun geestelijke aanwezigheid is nog altijd voelbaar. Francine en Kees waren niet de oppervlakkige types. Bijgevolg werden ze zelden afgeschrikt door de wisselvalligheid van het leven; ze realiseerden zich dat kennis de kracht is om in overvloed een nuttig leven te leiden, en dat deden ze.